Venus in Boston
A Romance of City Life

by

George Thompson

Venus in Boston
A Romance of City Life
by George Thompson

Copyright © 2024

All Rights reserved.

No part of this publication may be reproduced, stored in a retrieval system, or transmitted in any form or by any means, electronic, mechanical, photocopying or Otherwise, without the written permission of the publisher.
The author/editor asserts the moral right to be identified as the author/editor of this work.

ISBN: 978-93-68093-64-0

Published by

DOUBLE 9 BOOKS

2/13-B, Ansari Road
Daryaganj, New Delhi – 110002
info@double9books.com
www.double9books.com
Tel. 011-40042856

This book is under public domain

ABOUT THE AUTHOR

George Thompson was a writer known for his exploration of social issues, morality, and the complexities of urban life. His most notable work is Venus in Boston: A Romance of City Life, a novel that delves into the exploitation of vulnerable individuals in the context of a rapidly industrializing and morally complex city. Thompson's writing often addressed themes of poverty, class disparity, and the moral struggles faced by his characters, particularly focusing on the lives of women in precarious social positions.

In Venus in Boston, Thompson critiques the social and economic inequalities of America, focusing on the character of Fanny Aubrey, a young, impoverished fruit vendor in Boston. Through Fanny's struggles, the novel exposes the dangers of urban life, especially for women, and highlights the tension between innocence and societal corruption. The narrative also touches on themes of virtue, resilience, and the desire for social mobility in a world rife with exploitation. His works, especially Venus in Boston, offer valuable insight into the moral and social concerns of his era. His stories contributed to the broader tradition of social realism in American literature.

CONTENTS

Introduction 8

Chapter I
The blind Basket-maker and his family 9

Chapter II
Innocence in the Grip of Lust 14

Chapter III
The Rescue 27

Chapter IV
A night in Ann street 31

Chapter V
The Chevalier and the Duchess 75

Chapter VI
The Stolen Package.—The Midnight Outrage.—
The Marriage, and Awful Discovery 104

Chapter VII
Showing the operations of Jew Mike and his
coadjutors.—The necessity of young ladies
looking beneath their beds, before retiring to rest 122

Chapter VIII
The Chambers of Love.—Conclusion 133

Conclusion 140

"Ah, Vice! how soft are thy voluptuous ways!
While boyish blood is mantling,
who can 'scape The fascination of thy magic gaze?
A Cherub-hydra round us dost thou gape,
And mould to every taste,
thy dear, delusive shape."

                BYRON'S CHILDE HAROLD

Introduction

I conceive it to be a prominent fault of most of the tales of fiction that are written and published at the present day, that they are not sufficiently *natural*—their style is too much exaggerated—and in aiming to produce startling effects, they depart too widely from the range of probability to engage the undivided interest of the enlightened and judicious reader. Believing as I do that the romance of reality—the details of common, everyday life—the secret history of things hidden from the public gaze, but of the existence of which there can be no manner of doubt—are endowed with a more powerful and absorbing interest than any extravagant flight of imagination can be, it shall be my aim in the following pages to adhere as closely as possible to truth and reality; and to depict scenes and adventures which have actually occurred, and which have come to my knowledge in the course of an experience no means limited—an experience replete with facilities for acquiring a perfect insight into human nature, and a knowledge of the many secret springs of human action.

The most favorable reception which my former humble productions have met with, at the hands of a kind and indulgent public, will, I trust, justify the hope that the present Tale may meet with similar encouragement. It certainly shall not prove inferior to any of its predecessors in the variety of its incidents or the interest of its details; and as a *romance of city life*, it will amply repay the perusal of all country readers, as well as those who reside in cities.

With these remarks, preliminary and explanatory, I proceed at once to draw the curtain, and unfold the opening scene of my drama.

Chapter I
The blind Basket-maker and his family

It was a winter's day, and piercing cold; very few pedestrians were to be seen in Boston, and those few were carefully enveloped in warm cloak and great coats, for the weather was of that intense kind that chills the blood and penetrates to the very bone. Even Washington street—that great avenue of wealth and promenade of fashion, usually thronged with the pleasure-seeking denizens of the metropolis—was comparatively deserted, save by a few shivering mortals, who hurried on their way with rapid footsteps, anxious to escape from the relentless and iron grasp of hoary winter. And yet on that day, and in that street, there stood upon the pavement directly opposite the "Old South Church," a young girl of about the age of fourteen years, holding in her hand a small basket of fruit, which she offered to every passer-by. Now there was nothing very extraordinary in this, neither was there anything very unusual in the meek and pleading look of the little fruit girl, as she timidly raised her large blue eyes to the face of every one who passed her—for such humble callings, and such mute but eloquent appeals, are the common inheritance of many, very many of God's poor in large cities, and do not generally attract any great degree of notice from the careless (and too often unfeeling) children of prosperity;—but there was something in the appearance of the pale, sad girl, as, in her scant attire she shivered in the biting wind, not often met with in the humble disciples of poverty—a certain subdued, gentle air, partaking of much unconscious grace, that whispered of better days gone by.

At length the clock in the steeple of the "Old South" pronounced that the dinner hour had arrived—and despite the intense cold, the street soon became alive with people hurrying to and fro; for what weather can induce a hungry man to neglect that important era in the events of the day—his *dinner*? This perfumed exquisite hurried by to fulfil an appointment and dine at Parker's; the more sober and economical citizen hastened on his way to "feed" at some establishment of less pretensions and more moderate prices; while the mass of the diners-out repaired to appease their hunger at the numerous cheap refectories that abound in the neighborhood. But the poor, forlorn little fruit girl stood unnoticed by the passing throng, which like the curtain of a river hurried by, leaving her upon its margin, a neglected, drooping flower.

"Ah," she murmured—"why will they not buy my fruit? I have not taken a single penny to-day, and how can I return home to poor grandfather and my little brother, without food? Good people, could you but see them, your hearts would be softened—." And the tears rolled down her cheeks.

While thus soliloquizing, she had not noticed the approach of a little old man, in a faded, threadbare suit, and with a care-worn, wrinkled countenance. He stopped short when he saw that she was weeping, and in an abrupt, yet not unkind manner, inquired—

"My child, why do you weep?"

The girl looked up through her tears at the stranger, and in a few artless words related her simple story. She was an orphan, and with her little brother, lived with her grandfather. They were very poor, and were wholly dependent upon a small pittance which the grandfather (who was blind) daily earned by basket making, together with the very small profits which she realized by the sale of fruit in the streets. Her grandfather was very ill, and unable to work, and the poor family had not tasted food that day.

"Poor thing!" exclaimed the little old man when she had concluded her affecting narrative. He straightaway began fumbling in his pockets, and it seemed with no very satisfactory result, for he muttered—"The devil! I have no money—not a copper; bah! I can give you nothing. But hold! where do you live, my child?"

The girl stated her place of residence, which was in an obscure but respectable section of the city. The little old man produced a greasy memorandum book, and a stump of a pencil, with which he noted down the direction; then, uttering a grunt of satisfaction, but without saying a single word, he resumed his walk, and was soon lost in the crowd.

Evening came, and with it a furious snow-storm. Madly the wind careered through the streets—now fiercely dashing the snow into the faces of such unfortunate travellers as chanced to be abroad in that wild weather—now shaking the roofs of crazy old houses—and now tearing away in the distance with a howl of triumph at its power. The storm fiend was abroad—the elements were at war, and yet in the midst of that furious tumult, the poor fruit girl was toiling on her way towards her humble home. She reached it at last. It was a poor and lowly place, the abode of humble but decent poverty; yet the angel of peace had spread her wings there, and contentment had sat with them at their frugal board. True, it was but a garret; yet that little family, with hearts united by holy love, felt that to them it was a *home*. And then its little window commanded a distant view of a shining river, and green, pleasant fields beyond; and all day long, in fine weather, the cheerful sunshine looked in upon them, casting a gleam of gladness upon their hearts. It had been a happy home to the blind basket-maker and his grandchildren; but alas! sickness had laid its heavy hand upon the aged man, and want and wretchedness had become their portion.

The girl entered with a sad heart, for she brought no relief to the hungering and sorrowing inmates of that lowly dwelling. Without saying a word she seated herself at the bed-side of her grandfather, and taking his hand in hers, bedewed it with her tears. The old man turned towards her, and said—

"Thou art weeping, Fanny—what distresses thee? Tears are for the aged and the sorrowing—not for the young. Thou hast not brought us food?—well, well; the will of Heaven be done! I shall soon be in the grave, and then thou and Charley—"

"No, no, grandfather, pray don't say so," cried the poor girl, sobbing as if her heart would break—"what should we do without you? Heaven may spare you many happy years. I can work for you, and—"

"So can I, too," rejoined her brother Charley, a lad eight or nine years of age—"and only to-day I got a promise from Mr. Scott the tailor, that I might, when a little older, run of errands for him, and my wages will be a dollar and a half a week—only think how much money I shall earn!"

"Thou art a brave little man," said the grandfather—"but, my children, let us put our trust in God, and if it is His will that my earthly pilgrimage should end, be it so! Thank Heaven, I owe nothing, and can die at peace with all the world."

It had long been Fanny's custom to occupy an hour or so every evening, in reading to her grandfather. But that evening she did not, as usual, draw up the little table, and open the pages of some well-thumbed, ancient volume, to read, for perhaps the twentieth time, of the valorous deeds of some famed knight of the olden time, or mayhap, of the triumphant death of some famed martyr for religion's sake. For alas! the frugal but wholesome meal which had always preceded the reading of those ancient chronicles, was now wanting; and the little family sat listening to the raging of the pitiless storm without and counting the weary moments as they passed.

The bell in a neighboring steeple had just told the hour of nine, when, as the echo of that last stroke died away in the distance, a heavy step was heard ascending the stairs that led to their humble apartment. As the sound approached nearer, Fanny heard a voice occasionally giving utterance to expressions of extreme irritation and impatience, accompanied by certain sounds indicating that the person, whoever it might be, often stumbled upon the dark, narrow and somewhat dilapidated stair-case. "Blood and bomb-shells!" exclaimed a voice—"I shall never reach the top, and my shins are broken. The devil! there I go again. Corporal Grimsby, thou art an ass, and these stairs are the devil's trap!" And here the luckless unknown paused a moment to breathe, rub his shins, and refresh himself with an emphatic imprecation upon all dark and broken stair-cases in general, but upon *that* one in particular. At this moment, Fanny made her appearance at the landing with a light, and was astonished to behold her new acquaintance of that afternoon, the little old man who had inquired her residence. A most rueful expression sat upon his visage, and he carried upon one arm a huge basket. The friendly light enabled him soon to reach the end of his journey; he entered the little room without ceremony, and depositing his burden upon the table, exclaimed—

"Hark'ee, child, I am an old soldier, am not apt to grumble at trifles, [*illegible word*] and blunderbusses! I never before got into such a snarl.—Mounting the ramparts of the enemy was mere child's play to it!" Here he began to take out the contents of the basket, meanwhile keeping up a running commentary, during which his countenance wore an expression of the most intense ill-humor, in strange contrast with the evident benevolence of his character and intentions. He found fault with everything which he had brought, although, in truth, the articles were all of excellent quality.

"Here," said he, with a growl of dissatisfaction—"is a pair of chickens—starved, skinny imps, for which I paid double their value to that knave of a poultry merchant—bah! And here are some French rolls, that I'll be sworn are as hard as the French cannon balls that were thrown at Austerlitz. These vegetables are well enough, and this pastry hath a savory smell, but pistols and cutlasses! this wine *looks* as sour as General Grouty's face on a grand parade. Let me draw the cork and taste—no, by the nose of Napoleon! it is excellent—fit for the great Frederick himself. Here, child, haste and spread a cloth, for I am hungrier than a Cossack. Powder and shot! we shall have a supper fit for a Field Marshal!"

By this time the eccentric but kind old man had placed upon the table all the materials of an excellent and substantial repast. This done, he turned to the grandfather of Fanny, who had listened to his speech with much astonishment, and exclaimed—

"Cheer thee up, old friend, cheer thee up, and pick a bone with us; here, wash the cobwebs from thy throat by a hearty draught from this flask. I am an old soldier, and love all men; I stand on no ceremony; so fall to, fall to!"

Saying this, he seated himself at the table, and having seen that all were duly supplied with a liberal portion of the edibles, commenced the attack with [*illegible word*] truly surprising. Nor were the others at all backward in emulating so good an example. The grandfather, whose illness had mainly been produced by a lack of those little luxuries so essential to the debilities and infirmities of advanced age, after partaking sparingly of what was set before him, felt himself much bettered and refreshed thereby; and Fanny, who had dried her tears, and satisfied the cravings of hunger, smiled her gratitude upon the kind provider. Little Charley had already become much attached to "good Corporal Grimsby," who had given him such a nice supper—while the latter gentleman, having finished his meal, drew forth an antiquated pipe, having a Turk's head for the bowl and a coiled serpent for the stem, which having lighted, he proceeded to smoke with much gravity and thoughtfulness. Not a word did he utter, but smoked away in silence, until the clock struck ten; then pocketing his pipe, and depositing the now empty flask and dishes in the basket, he announced his intention of departing. The grandfather was cut short in a grateful acknowledgment of the stranger's kindness, by the abrupt exit of that singular personage, who bolted down stairs with a precipitancy that was truly alarming, scarce waiting for Fanny to light him down.

This singular visit was of course the subject of much surprise and conjecture in the little family of the blind basket-maker; but when Fanny related how the stranger had accosted her in the street, and inquired her residence, they concluded that he was some eccentric but benevolent person, who had taken that method of contributing to the relief of their wants.

And who was this queer little old man, so shabby and threadbare—so "full of strange oaths,"—so odd in his manner, so kind in his heart—calling himself Corporal Grimsby—who had come forward at that opportune moment to supply a starving family with food? Time will show.

Chapter II
Innocence in the Grip of Lust

The day which succeeded the stormy night described in the last chapter, was an unusually fine one. The sun shone clear and bright, and many people were abroad to enjoy the fine bracing air, and indemnify themselves for having been kept within doors on the preceding day. The streets were covered with an ample garment of snow, and the merry music of the sleigh-bells was heard in every direction.

At an early hour, Fanny Aubrey (for that was the name of our little heroine,) issued from her dwelling, and taking the sunny side of the streets, resumed her accustomed perambulations, with her basket on her arm. Fanny was small for her age, but exceedingly pretty; her eyes were of a dark blue—her hair a rich auburn—her features radiant with the inexpressible charm of youth and innocence. I have said that her air was superior to her condition; in truth, every motion of hers had in it a certain winning grace, and her step was light as a fawn's, although her figure was not without a certain degree of plumpness, which gave ample promise of a speedy voluptuous development. Though plumpness in the female figure is considered to be incompatible with perfect grace, I agree with those who regard it as decidedly preferable to an excessive thinness, though the latter be accompanied with the lightness of a zephyr, and the grace of a sylph.

Dress is sometimes acknowledged to be a sign of character—and the dress of Fanny Aubrey certainly indicated the native refinement of her mind—for though poor in material and faded by long use, it was well put on and scrupulously neat—indeed, there was something almost coquettish in the style of her bonnet and the arrangement of her scanty shawl—too scanty, alas! to shield her adequately from the inclemency of the weather.

As she passed along the street, her beauty and prepossessing appearance attracted the attention of many gay loiterers, who regard her with various feelings of admiration, pity and surprise that one so lovely should pursue so humble an occupation; nor were there wanting many well-dressed libertines, young and old, who gazed with eyes of lustful desire upon the fair young creature, evidently so unprotected and so poor.

Reader, pardon us if for one brief moment we pause to contemplate the black and hideous character of THE SEDUCER. Should the teeming hosts of hell's dominions meet in grand convention, amid the mysterious darkness and lurid flames of their eternal abode—should that infernal conclave of murderers, robbers, monsters of iniquity, perpetrators of damning crimes; possessors of black hearts and polluted souls on earth, whose mighty sins had sunk them in that burning pit—should all those lost spirits select from among their number, *one fiend*, the worst of them all, to represent them *all* on earth—unite within his being *all* the crimes of which they had collectively been guilty—to show mankind how vast and stupendous have been *all* the sins perpetrated since the creation of the globe—*that fiend* could not cast a blacker shadow upon human nature than doth the seducer of female innocence. Oh! if there be one wretch living who deserves to be cast forth from the society of his fellow men—if there be one who deserves to be trod on as a venomous insect, and crushed as the vilest reptile that crawls—it is he who calmly and deliberately sets himself about the hellish task of accomplishing the ruin of a weak, confiding woman—and then, having sipped the sweets and inhaled the fragrance of the flower, tramples it beneath his feet. Will not the thunderbolts of Omnipotent wrath shatter the perjured soul of such a villain?

But to resume. Fanny Aubrey pursued her walk, and was so fortunate as to escape the insults (except such as were conveyed in glances,) of the many libertines who are ever ready to take advantage of a female in a situation like hers. As she was passing a magnificent mansion in a quarter of the city mainly occupied by the residences of the aristocracy, a beautiful young lady alighted from a splendid sleigh, and observing the little fruit girl, beckoned her to approach. Fanny modestly complied, and the young lady, with one of the sweetest smiles imaginable selected an orange from her basket, and taking out a purse, presented her with a bright gold coin.

"I have no change, Miss," said Fanny, in some confusion.

"Keep the money, my poor girl," rejoined the young lady, with a look of deep compassion, as a tear of pity dimmed her bright eyes—"I am sure you need it; you are much too pretty for such an employment. If you will try and pass this way to-morrow at about this time, you may see me again."

Amid Fanny's heartfelt thanks, the young lady entered the mansion, and the door was closed.

Poor Fanny! she resumed her journey with a light heart. She never before had possessed so much money. Five dollars! the sum seemed inexhaustible, and she began to devise a thousand plans to expend it to advantage—and the fact that she herself was not included in any of those plans, was a beautiful illustration of the unselfishness of her character. Not for a moment did she dream of appropriating it to the purchase of a good warm shawl or dress for herself, although, poor girl! she so much needed both. She would buy a nice comfortable rocking-chair for her grandfather; or a thick great-coat for little Charley—she couldn't make up her mind which, she loved them both so much—yet when she thought of the poor, sick, blind old man, a holy pity triumphed over sisterly affection, and she resolved upon the rocking-chair. Then she determined to hasten homewards to communicate her good fortune to her friends; and on her way she could not help thinking of the beautiful young lady who had given her the money, of her sweet smile, and the kind words she had spoken; and wondered if she should really see her again the next day. These thoughts, and the hope of seeing her benefactress again, made her feel very happy; and she was hastening towards her home with a glad heart, when her footsteps were arrested by a crowd of those dissolute young females, who pervade every section of the city, and are universally known as "apple girls."

These girls are usually from ten to fifteen years of age, and are proverbial for their vicious propensities and dishonesty. Under pretence of selling their fruit, they are accustomed to penetrate into the business portions of the city particularly; and in doing this they have two objects in view. In the first place, if on entering an office or place of business, they find nobody in, an opportunity is afforded them for plunder; and it is needless to say they are ever ready to steal and carry off whatever they can lay their hands on. Secondly, these girls have been brought up in vice from their infancy; they are, for the most part, neither more nor less than common prostitutes, and will freely yield their persons to whoever will pay for the same.—Should the merchant, or lawyer, or man of business, into whose office one of these "apple girls" may chance to intrude, solicit her favors (and there are many miscreants, *respectable* ones, too, who do this, as we shall show,) and offer her a small pecuniary reward, he has only to lock his door and draw his curtains, to accomplish his object without the slightest difficulty. Thus, their ostensible employment of selling fruit is nothing but a cloak for their real trade of prostitution and thieving. The profanity and obscenity of their conversation alone, is a sufficient evidence of their true character.

The girls whom we have mentioned as having encountered Fanny on her return home, were a squalid and dirty set, though several of them were not destitute of good looks, as far as form and features were concerned. They surrounded her with many a fierce oath and ribald jest, and it was easy to see that they were jealous of her superior cleanliness of person and respectability of character.

"Ha, ha!" cried one, a dirty-faced wench of thirteen, clutching Fanny fiercely by the arm, while the poor girl stood afraid and trembling in the midst of that elfish crew—"ha, ha! here is my fine lady, with her smooth face and clean gown, who disdains to keep company with us, and do as we do! Let us tear off her clothes, and roll her in the mire!"

They were proceeding to act upon this suggestion, when Fanny, bewildered and speechless with terror, dropped her gold coin, which she held in her hand, upon the ground. It was instantly snatched up by one of the gang, who was immediately attacked by the others, and a fierce struggle ensued, for the possession of the coin, the young wretches tearing, scratching and biting each other like so many wild cats. During this conflict, Fanny made off as fast as she could run, but was followed and overtaken by one of the gang, a large girl of fifteen, who was known among her companions by the pleasing title of "Sow Nance." She was a thief and prostitute of the most desperate and abandoned character, hideously ugly in person, and of a disposition the most ferocious and deceitful.—Laying her brawny hand upon Fanny's shoulder, she said, in a hoarse and croaking voice—

"See here, Miss What's-yer-name, I wants to speak to you, if you please. You needn't be afraid of me, for I won't hurt you. Them thieving hussies has got your money, and you must make up your loss the best way you can. Look at my basket—you see it's empty, don't yer? I've sold all my fruit already, and if you'll go with me, I'll show you a nice gentleman who will buy all the fruit in your little basket, and pay you well, too. It's not far—will you go with me?"

The prospect of effecting a speedy sale of her stock in trade, was too tempting to be resisted by poor Fanny, especially in view of the severe loss she had just sustained, in being robbed of the money which the kind young lady had given her. She therefore gladly consented to accompany Sow Nance to the nice gentleman who would pay her so well for the contents of her basket.

Poor, innocent, unsuspecting Fanny! she little thought that the abandoned creature at her side was leading her into a snare, imminently dangerous to her peace of mind and future happiness! "I will save up money enough to buy grandfather a rocking-chair, after all," thought she, as she gaily trudged onward, while ever and anon Sow Nance would glare savagely at her from the corners of her snake-like eyes. It is one of the worst qualities peculiar to corrupt human nature, the hatred with which the wicked and abandoned regard the innocent and pure. Fanny had never in the slightest degree injured the wretch who was plotting her ruin;—and Sow Nance had no other reason for hating her, than because she herself was a guilty and polluted being, while Fanny she knew to be without stain or blemish.

In about a quarter of an hour they reached a handsome brick house in South street.

"This is the place," said Sow Nance, as she rang the door bell; the summons was immediately answered by an old negro woman, who, exchanging a significant look with Nance, admitted them, and ushered them into a large parlor. The apartment was handsomely furnished, the walls adorned with many pictures, and the floor covered with a very rich carpet.

"Sit down, young ladies, and I will call Mr. Tickels down," said the old negro woman, as she left the room; in a few moments, a gentleman entered, and regarded Fanny with a gaze so piercing, that the poor girl was covered with confusion.

The gentleman was, to all appearances, full sixty years of age; he was a large, portly man, with very gray hair and a very red face: he was attired in a dressing-gown and slippers, and wore a magnificent diamond pin in his shirt frill.

This man was one of those wealthy beasts whose lusts run riot on the innocence of young females—whose crimes outnumbered the gray hairs upon his head, and whose riches were devoted to no other purpose than the procurement of victims for his appetite, and the gratification of his abominable passions.

A vague, strange fear stole over Fanny, while this gentleman thus viewed her so closely—a fear which she could not define, yet which rendered her excessively uneasy. Apparently the survey was satisfactory to the gentleman—for he smiled, and in doing so displayed two rows of teeth not unlike the fangs of a wolf. Then he beckoned Sow Nance to follow him from the room, and held a whispered conversation with her in the passage.

"Who is she, Nance?" asked the gentleman.

"Not *one of us*," was the reply, "she sells fruit, and is poor, but her folks are respectable;—you must pay me well for bringing her here, for she's handsome."

"True; but are you sure she has never—"

"*Sure!*" replied Nance, almost fiercely—"I'll take my oath on it; hasn't she always kept away from us, and ain't all the girls hating her like h——l, 'cause she's virtuous? Don't you suppose *I* know?"

"Good," said the gentleman; and taking a gold coin from his pocket, he gave it to Nance, who, stooping down, secreted it in her stocking; then she noiselessly opened the front door and left the house, singing in a hoarse voice, as she sped on her way towards Ann street, (where she lived,) these barbarous words:—

"The lamb to the wolf is sold, sold, sold;
No more she'll return to her fold, fold, fold—
And Sow Nance will dare another to snare,
And the wolf shall have her for gold, gold, gold!"

The gentleman (I use the word *ironically*, reader,) re-entered the parlor, advanced to where Fanny was seated, and laying his heavy hand upon the young girl's shoulder, glued his polluted lips to her pure cheek. She sprang from his profaning grasp with a cry of terror, and fled towards the door—it was *locked*! The gentleman laughed, and said—

"No, no, my pretty bird, you cannot escape from your cage so easily; and why should you wish to? Your cage shall have golden wires, and you shall be fed on delicacies, my little flutterer—so smooth the feathers of your bright wings, my dear, and sing your sweetest notes!"

Fanny burst into tears, and fell on her knees before the old libertine.— Young and innocent as she was, a dark suspicion of his purpose came like a shadow over her soul, and she cried in piteous accents—

"Pray, good sir, let me go home to my poor grandfather and my little brother—they will be expecting me, and will feel worried at my absence. Surely, sir, you will not have the heart to harm me—I am but a poor fruit girl, without father or mother. Pray let me go, sir."

That appeal, made touching by the youth and innocence of the speaker, and by her profound distress, might have melted a heart of iron—but it moved not the stony heart of the old villain, and he looked upon her with his cold, hard eyes, and his disgusting smile, as he said—

"Your tears make you doubly interesting, my sweet child. I am afraid that your poor grandfather and your little brother, as you call them, will be obliged to wait a long while for your return, let them worry ever so much at your absence. You say truly that I have not the heart to harm you, a poor fruit girl,—no, I will make a lady of you; and as you have, you say, neither father nor mother, I will supply their place, my pretty dear, and be your *lover* into the bargain. Those coarse garments shall be changed for silks and satins,—that shining hair shall be made radiant with gems,—jewels shall sparkle on that fair neck, and on those taper fingers,—you shall ride in a carriage, and have servants to wait on you,—and you shall sleep on a downy bed, and live in a grand house, like this. Say, will not all these fine things be better than selling fruit in the cold streets?"

But the sobbing girl implored him to let her go home. The gentleman ground his teeth with rage.

"Well, well," said he, after a brief pause, and speaking in an assumed tone of kindness, "you *shall* go home, since you wish it." He rang a bell, and the old negro woman appeared, to whom he whispered for a few moments, and then left the room.

"Come, Miss," said the old wench, addressing Fanny, with a grin that was anything but encouraging or expressive of a friendly feeling—"come with me up stairs, and wash the tears from your pretty face; then you shall go home—ha, ha, ha!"

It was a demon's laugh, full of malice and hatred; yet Fanny smiled through her tears, for she saw not the old wretch's malignity, and only thought of her escape from the danger which had menaced her, and anticipated the happiness she should feel when once more in safety beneath her own humble roof, in the society of all she held dear on earth. Joyfully did she follow the old wench up stairs and into an apartment still more handsomely furnished than the one below; but what was her astonishment and affright, when her sable conductress gave her a violent push which threw her violently to the floor, and then quickly left the room and locked the door! A presentiment that she was imprisoned, and for the worst of purposes, flashed through her mind, and she made the apartment resound with her shrieks. But, alas! no help was near—no friendly hand was there to burst open the door of her prison, and rescue her from a house, within whose walls she was threatened with the worst fate that can befall a helpless maiden—the loss of her honor. Her loud shrieks penetrated not beyond the precincts of that massive building—her calls for help were answered only by the taunting laugh of the black hag outside, who loaded her with alternate abuse, threats, and curses. At last, exhausted and despairing, poor Fanny threw herself upon the carpet, and prayed—oh, how earnestly!—that no harm might happen to her, which could call the blush of shame to her cheek, or make her poor grandfather think of her as a lost, polluted thing.

Somewhat relieved by this, (and who shall say that a holy whisper breathed not into her pure heart the assurance that she should pass unscathed through the fiery furnace?) she arose with a calmer spirit, and began to survey the apartment in which she was confined. It was a large room, very elegantly furnished, containing a piano, and a profusion of paintings. On examining one of these, Fanny turned away with a burning cheek—for it was one of those immodest productions of the French school, which show how art and talent can be perverted to the basest uses. She looked at no more of the pictures, but went to a window and looked out. The view from thence was not extensive, but merely included a garden of moderate size, surrounded by a high wall; the prospect was not a pleasant one, for instead of blooming flowers, the appropriate divinities of such a place, nothing was to be seen but a smooth surface of snow, relieved here and there by gaunt trees, whose leafless branches waved mournfully in the breeze, seeming to sing a requiem for the departed summer.

Fanny turned sadly away from this gloomy prospect, and seating herself upon a luxurious sofa, abandoned herself to the melancholy reflections engendered by her situation. Soon the fortitude which she had summoned to her aid, deserted her, and as the increasing darkness of the room betokened the approach of night, a thousand fears chilled her heart. She was alone in that strange house—no friends were near—the treatment she had received from the gentleman and his negro menial, indicated that neither of them would hesitate to do her mischief, if they were so inclined— what if they should murder her—or, dreadful thought! first outrage, and then despatch her! While employed in such terrible meditations as these, the darkness increased; grim shadows hovered around, and dim but terrific shapes seemed to glide towards the trembling girl. She groped her way towards the window, and looked out—there was no moon, and not a star glimmered in the firmament. Soon the darkness grew so intense, that had she held her hand close to her eyes, she could not have seen it.

Every moment augmented her fears; and sinking down in one corner, she pressed her hands to her aching eyes, as if to shut out some hideous spectacle.

Not long had she been thus, when a mortal terror, to which all her other fears were as nothing, seized her; she shivered with horror, and cold perspiration started from every pore of her skin—for her sense of hearing, painfully acute, detected the presence of a *moving object* in the room—she heard the rustle of garments—a footstep—the sound of breathing; she strained her eyes through the intense darkness, but could distinguish nothing. The moving object approaching her, nearer and nearer—it seemed to be groping in search of her—and her blood froze with horror when at last a cold hand touched her cheek, and she beheld a pair of eyes glaring at her through the gloom. A low, mocking laugh—a whispered curse—and the object glided away; then Fanny lost all consciousness.

When she recovered from the swoon into which she had fallen, daylight was shining through the windows. Hours passed away, and no one came to invade the girl's solitude. At about noon, the door was unlocked, and the old negro woman appeared, bearing a plate of provisions and a basket full of clothing. Placing the food before Fanny, the hag bade her eat, a request readily complied with, as she had fasted since the preceding day. While she was eating, the old negress regarded her with a hideous grin, and eyes expressing all the malignity of a serpent; and at the conclusion of the repast, asked her—

"Well, Miss, how did you pass the night?"

Fanny related the fearful visitation she had experienced, and implored to be released from her confinement; the black woman laughed disdainfully.

"No, no, Miss," said she, "my master will never let you go until of your own free will, you become his own little lady, and take him for a lover. Listen to me, girl: I am going to speak for your own good. My master is very fond of young ladies such as you, and goes to every expense to get them into the house; but he never likes to *force* them to his wishes, his delight being to have them *willing* to receive him as a lover—do you understand? But those silly girls who are *not* willing, he shuts up in this room, which is haunted by a fearful spectre, who every night visits the obstinate girl, and sometimes punishes her dreadfully, until she consents to my master's wishes."

Fanny shuddered—and the old black woman continued, in a gentler tone—

"Now won't you, to avoid this fearful spectre, consent to become my master's little lady? I am sure you will, my dear. See—I have brought you some fine clothes to wear, so that you may be fit to receive Mr. Tickels this afternoon, as he intends to visit you. Now, don't fail to be very good and kind to him, for he loves you very much, and will make a fine lady of you. Come, let us take off those old clothes, and put on this beautiful silk dress that has been bought on purpose for you."

We have so far depicted Fanny as a very timid, gentle girl; but she was not destitute of a becoming spirit.—When, therefore, she heard that old wretch so calmly and deliberately talk of her surrendering herself to dishonor and shame, the flush of indignation mantled her cheek; she arose, and boldly confronting her tormentor, said, with spirit and determination—

"I *will not* wear your fine clothes, nor become the slave of your master's will! He is a villain for keeping me here—and you are a wretch, a wicked wretch, for trying to tempt me to do wrong. I am not afraid of the spectre you speak of, for God will protect me, and keep me from harm. You may kill me, if you like, but I will not—*will not* be guilty of the wickedness you wish me to commit; and if ever I get free from this bad place, you and your master shall be made to suffer for treating me so. Remember this, you nasty old black devil—remember this!"

The negress quailed before the young girl, whose singular beauty was enhanced ten-fold by the glow of indignation on her cheek and the sparkle of anger in her eye. Then, without saying a word, she left the room, locking the door after her.

Half an hour elapsed, and the wench again made her appearance; in her hand she carried a short, stout piece of rope. With the fury of a tigress, and a countenance (black as she was) livid with rage, she flew at the young girl, tore every shred of clothing from her person, and then beat her cruelly with the rope, until her fair skin was covered in various places with black and blue marks. In vain poor Fanny implored for mercy; the black savage continued to beat her until obliged to desist by sheer exhaustion. Throwing herself breathless into a chair, she said, with a fierce oath—

"So, Miss—I'm a nasty old black devil, am I? You impudent hussy, how dare you use such language to me? But I'll learn you better. You shall be more civil, and do as my master wishes, and obey me in everything, or I'll not leave a whole bone in your skin. Now put on these new clothes instantly, or I solemnly swear I'll not leave off beating you, until you lie at my feet, a corpse!"

Poor Fanny was obliged to obey—for, apart from the black woman's threat, she had no alternative but to put on the costly garments which had been procured for her, her own clothes being torn to pieces; and of course she did not wish to remain in a state of nudity. She therefore dressed herself—and in truth, the garments were well selected, and fitted her to a charm. Even when attired in her old clothes, she had looked exceedingly pretty; but now, dressed in an elegant costume which displayed her fine shape and budding charms to the best advantage, she was positively beautiful. Even the old black woman could not help smiling with satisfaction at her improved appearance.

"She is a choice tit-bit for my master's appetite," thought she, chuckling to herself; and then she brought water, and made Fanny wash the traces of tears from her face, and arrange her rich auburn hair neatly and tastefully. This done, the negress departed, after telling the young girl to prepare to receive Mr. Tickels in the course of the afternoon.

What must have been the reflections of that poor young creature, while dreading the entrance of the hoary villain who sought her ruin? We can but imagine them: doubtless she thought with agony of her poor grandfather and little Charley, both of whom she knew would suffer all the anguish of uncertainty and fear, with reference to her fate. Then, perhaps, her mind reverted to the happiness she used to enjoy within the hallowed precincts of her humble home—which, humble as it was, and devoid of every luxury, and many comforts, was nevertheless endeared to her by a thousand tender associations, and had been to her as an ark of safety from the storms of life. Her thoughts next dwelt upon the kind young lady, who had given her the gold coin, and whose sweet smile and pitying words still lingered in her heart. And should she ever see those dear relatives or that kind friend again? Or if she did, would she be able to look them in the face as a pure and stainless girl, or would she blush in their presence with a consciousness of degradation? But she was interrupted in these painful meditations by the sound of the key turning in the lock; and a moment afterwards Mr. Tickels entered the room, and advanced towards her. On observing her improved appearance, a smile of intense satisfaction overspread his bloated face and sensual features—and his eyes rested admiringly upon her form, which, though not ripened, was beginning to assume a voluptuous fullness that betokened approaching womanhood. Taking her hand, he drew her to a sofa and seated her by his side. How tumultuously her heart beat with apprehension and fear!—and the old *gentleman's* first words were by no means calculated to allay her alarm.

"My charming little girl," said he, raising her hand to his lips—"how beautiful you look! A *fruit girl!*—by heavens, you are fit to be a duchess! Such sweet blue eyes—such luxuriant hair—such pure Grecian features—such a complexion, the rose blending with the lily—such a snowy breast, expanding into the two "apples of love!" And that little foot, peeping so coquettishly from beneath the skirts of your dress, should ever be encased in a satin slipper, and press naught but rich and downy carpets in the magnificent saloons of aristocratic wealth! Nay, nay, my little trembler, be not afraid, but listen to me: I love you more than words can express—you are the star of my life, and your lustre shall light me on my way to more than celestial felicity. Hear me still further: the world bows the knee to me because I am rich—thus do I kneel to you, my angel, for you are beautiful. You shall dwell with me in a mansion, to which, in point of splendor, this is nothing. I will have a *boudoir* prepared expressly for your use; it shall be lined with pink satin, and in summer the windows will overlook a beautiful garden, full of choice fruits and rare flowers; a sparkling fountain shall play in its centre, and your ears will be ravished with the melody of birds. You shall wander in that garden as much as you choose, and when you are tired, you shall repose in a shady arbor, and dream of love and its thousand blisses. In the winter season, like this, the opera, the ballroom, the theatre, shall minister to your pleasure; and in those places, none shall surpass you in splendor of dress or magnificence of jewels. Say, *belissima*, will you give me your love in exchange for all these things?"

While uttering the above wild rhapsody, (which is given at length in order to show the temptations with which the old libertine sought to allure his intended victim,) he had kneeled at her feet, and, despite her resistance, encircled her waist with his arm.

And did that poor girl—the daughter of poverty—the child of want—whose home was a garret, and who was familiar with the chills of winter and the cravings of hunger,—did she, while listening to the splendid promises of the rich man who knelt at her feet, for a moment waver in her pride of virtue, or even dream of accepting his brilliant offers? No! for even had she no other scruples, a host of holy memories encircled her heart, as a shield of power against the tempter's wiles,—the memory of home, of the two loved beings she had left there, of former happiness in a more elevated sphere; and of a gentle mother, whose beauty and virtues she had inherited, whose counsels she remembered, and who was sleeping in the churchyard.

Disengaging herself from the libertine's embrace, and thoroughly aroused to a sense of her danger, and the necessity of making all the resistance she was capable of, to preserve her chastity and honor, the young girl, losing all sense of fear, poured forth a torrent of indignant eloquence that for the time completely abashed and overcame the hoary and lecherous villain.

"No, sir—I will not, cannot love you; I hate and despise you, old wretch that you are, seeking to tempt a poor child like me to her ruin. Oh! you are rich, and have the manners of a gentleman before the world,—and yet you are more base, mean and cowardly than the commonest ruffian that ever stole a purse or cut a throat! Let me go hence, I command you; you dare not refuse me, for I know there is a law to protect *me*, as well as the richest and the highest, and I will go to those who execute the law, and have you dragged to the bar of justice to answer for this outrage. Do you hear, sir?—let me go from this accursed place, or dread the power of the law and the vengeance of Almighty God!"

The libertine quailed before the flashing eyes and proud scorn of his intended victim; his discomfiture, however, lasted but for a moment. His red face grew black with the passions of rage and lust combined; he muttered a fierce curse, and springing forward, seized her in his vice-like grasp, and forced her towards the sofa, exclaiming—

"Curses on you, little hell-bird, since neither persuasions nor promises will make you mine, it shall be done by force. Nay, if you scream so, by the powers of darkness I'll strangle you!"

In all human probability he would have been as good as his word, for Fanny continued to scream louder and louder; when suddenly Mr. Tickels received a blow on the head that brought him to the ground, and a voice cried out—

"Broad-swords and bomb-shells! I am just in time!"

While the libertine lay sprawling upon the carpet, Fanny turned to thank her deliverer; and what was her astonishment and joy when she beheld the wrinkled, care-worn face, and odd, shabby garments of—Corporal Grimsby.

Chapter III
The Rescue

"By the nose of Napoleon!" cried the worthy Corporal, clasping Fanny in his arms,—"this is fortunate. Attacked the enemy in the rear—drove him from his position,—completely routed him, and left him wounded on the field; and you, my dear child, are the spoils of war!"

Mr. Tickels arose with difficulty from his prostrate position, rubbing his forehead, which was decorated with a token of the Corporal's vigor, in the shape of a huge bump not included in the science of phrenology. Turning fiercely to the latter gentleman, and quivering with rage, he demanded—

"Death and fury, sir! how dare you intrude into this room,—into this house? Who are you, and what in the devil's name brings you here? Speak, you villain, or—"

"Hold!" cried the Corporal, his face crimsoning with anger, for he was a choleric little old gentleman, was the Corporal, and as quick to become enraged as to do a good action; "hold! No man shall call me villain with impunity; I shot two rascally Dons at Madrid for the same word, and by God, sir, if *you* repeat it, I'll cane you within an inch of your life!"

Mr. Tickels was as great a coward as a scoundrel; and though he was a much more powerful man than the Corporal, he deemed it prudent not to enrage the fierce little old gentleman more than necessary. He therefore adopted a milder tone, and asked,—

"Well, sir, what is your business here?"

"To convey this poor child to her home and friends," replied the Corporal, sternly. "It matters not how I ascertained her whereabouts; 'tis enough to know that I arrived here in time to rescue her from your brutality. You shall pay dearly for this outrage, damn you!" added the Corporal, again getting into a passion, and turning very red in the face. "But come, my child, let us leave the den of this old hyena, and go to your poor grandfather and little Charley."

Mr. Tickels closed the door, and placed his back against it with a determined air.

"You are mistaken, sir," said he, calmly,—"if you suppose that you can thus force yourself into my house, and into my private apartments, and without explanation kidnap or carry off a young person whose presence here is no affair of yours. Do you know me, sir? I am the Honorable Timothy Tickels, ex-member of Congress, men are not in the habit of questioning my motives or interfering with my actions. I am rich, and my influence is unbounded, and, were I so disposed, I could have you severely punished for the assault which you have committed on me. Your dress and appearance indicate poverty, although your language evinces that you have enjoyed more elevated fortunes; I am disposed to be not only merciful, but generous. Come, sir—leave this young person with me, unmolested; depart from this house quietly, and say nothing about what you have seen, and here is a fifty dollar bill for you. When you need more, come to me, and you shall have it."

The Honorable Mr. Tickels drew from his well-filled wallet a bank-note for the amount named, and handed it to the Corporal, who regarded it with a curious smile, and twirled it in his fingers. His smile may have been one of gratification at receiving the money—but it looked very much like a sneer of contempt for the donor and his bribe.

"Now is it not strange," quoth the Corporal, soliloquizing,—"that this dirty little bit of paper—its intrinsic value not one cent, its representative value fifty dollars,—is it not strange, I say, that this flimsy trifle, that an instant's application to the sickly flame of a penny candle would destroy, can procure food for the starving, clothing for the naked, shelter for the homeless? Great is thy power, money!—thou art the key to many of earth's pleasures,—the magic wand, which can summon a host of delights to gild the existence of thy votaries; thou cans't buy roses to strew life's rugged pathway—but thou cans't not, O great deity at whose shrine all men kneel, thou cans't not cleanse the polluted soul, still the troubled conscience, or dim the pure surface of unsullied honor. Nor cans't thou purchase *me*, thou sordid dross. Guns and grappling-irons!" abruptly added the Corporal, abandoning his philosophical strain, and getting into a towering passion,— "would you bribe me to desert my post as a guardian of innocence, and turn traitor to every principle of honor in my heart?—Bah!" and crumpling the bill in his hand, he threw it into the face of the Honorable Mr. Tickels, much to that individual's amazement.

"What do you mean, sir?" he demanded, "do you scorn my gift?"

"Yes!" thundered the little Corporal, "you and your gift may go to the devil together; and hark'ee, sir, perhaps 'tis well that you should know who *I* am, as you have so formally introduced yourself to me; I am—"

The remainder of the sentence was whispered in the ear of his listener, but the effect was magical. The Honorable Mr. Tickels started, and rapidly surveyed the person and countenance of the Corporal; then he reddened with confusion, and began to murmur a broken apology for his conduct, in which he was interrupted rather abruptly.

"Not a word, sir, not a word," said the little old gentleman, "all your apologies cannot remove from my mind the impression created by your treatment of this poor child; and, sir," (here the Corporal again lost his temper) "you cannot destroy my conviction that you are the d— —dest scoundrel that ever went unhung! Consider yourself fortunate if you are not held legally responsible for your forcible detention of the young girl in your house, and for your attempted outrage on her person,—damn you! Come, my child, this gentleman will no longer oppose our exit from his mansion."

The Corporal was right; the Honorable Mr. Tickels offered not the slightest objection to their departure, but on the contrary ushered them down stairs with great politeness, and held open the street door for them to pass out.

When Fanny found herself once more in the open street, out of the power of her persecutor, and on the way to her home and friends, her gratitude to her deliverer knew no bounds; she thanked the good Corporal a thousand times, and spoke of the approaching meeting with her grandfather and brother with rapture. Soon they reached their place of destination; once more the young girl stood in the humble apartment wherein all her affections were centered;—once more her aged grandfather clasped her in his arms, and again did she receive the fond kiss of fraternal love from the lips of her brother.

As soon as they had left the residence of the Honorable Mr. Tickels, in South street, the gentleman locked himself up in his study, threw himself into a chair, and actually began tearing his hair with rage and vexation.

"Hell and furies!" cried he—"to be thus fooled and baffled at the very moment when my object was about to be accomplished—to have that luscious morsel snatched from my grasp, when I was just about to taste its sweets. The thought is madness! And, in the name of wonder, how came HE to know that she was here, and why does *he* interest himself in her at all? I dare not trifle with *him*! Were some poor, poverty-stricken devil to constitute himself her champion, I might crush him at once; but *he* is above my reach. No matter; she shall yet be mine—I swear it, by all the powers of hell! I care not whether by open violence, or secret abduction, or subtle stratagem; I shall gain possession of her person, and once in my power, not all the angels in heaven, or men on earth, or fiends in hell, shall tear her from my grasp.—Ah, by Beelzebub, well tho't of!—I know the mistress of a house of prostitution (of which house I am the *owner*,) beneath whose den, as she has often told me, there is a secret cellar, which she has had privately constructed, and to which there is no access except through a panel in her chamber—which panel and the method of opening it, are known only to her, and a few persons in whom she can place implicit confidence.—This brothel-keeper told me, too, that she had the cellar made as a safe depository for young females who had been abducted from their homes,—a place of security from the search of friends, and the police. In that subterranean retreat, (which she informed me, is luxuriantly furnished, although the light of day never penetrates there,) these stolen girls are compelled to receive the visits of their lovers; and there, amid the gloom and silence of that underground prison they are initiated in all the mysteries of prostitution. By heaven 'tis the very place for my little fruit girl; she shall be abducted and conveyed there—and once safely lodged in these secret "Chambers of Love," HE who spoiled by sport to-day, shall in vain search for her. Let him come, bringing with him the myrmidons of the law; and let them search my house—then let them, if they choose, go to the brothel, beneath the foundation of which the girl is hidden, and search *that* house, too,—ha, ha, ha! They will search for her in vain. But *how* to abduct her—there's the rub! Tush! when did my ingenuity ever fail me, when appetite was to be fed or revenge gratified? Courage, Timothy Tickels, courage! Thy star, though dim at present, shall soon be in the ascendant!"

Such were the reflections of the old libertine, as he sat in his study after the departure of the Corporal and Fanny; and he was so delighted at the thought of a safe asylum for the latter, that, with restored good humor he applied himself to the discussion of a bottle of wine, and then, stretching himself comfortably on a sofa, fell asleep and dreamed of the subterranean "Chamber of Love," and the little fruit girl.

Chapter IV
A night in Ann street

We proceed now to show how the Corporal discovered the fact that Fanny Aubrey was confined in the mansion of the Honorable Mr. Tickels, in South street.

Great was the consternation and alarm of the blind basket-maker and little Charley, as the day passed away and evening came on, without the return of Fanny. They were agitated with a thousand fears for her safety, for both their lives were bound up in hers, and they doted on her with an affection rendered doubly ardent by their poverty and almost complete isolation from the world. In the midst of their distress, Corporal Grimsby entered, bringing, as on the evening before, a basket of provisions. To him they communicated the intelligence that Fanny had not returned; and the eccentric old man, without waiting to hear the recital of their fears, threw the basket on the table, bolted precipitately down stairs, and walked away towards Ann street with a rapidity that betokened the existence of some fixed purpose in his mind. Meanwhile, his reflections ran somewhat in the following strain, and were half muttered aloud, as he trudged quickly onward, now nearly upsetting a foot passenger and receiving a malediction on his awkwardness, and then bruising his unlucky shins against lampposts and other street fixtures.

"By the nose of Napoleon! what can have become of the little minx? lost or stolen?—most probably the latter, for in this infernal city a pretty girl like her, so unprotected and so poor, can no more traverse the streets with safety, than can a fine fat goose waddle into the den of a wolf unharmed. Curses on these lampposts, I am always breaking my neck against them—bah! Well, to consider: but why the devil do I interest myself in this little girl at all? Is it because I am a lonely, solitary old codger, with neither chick nor child to bless me with their love, and whom I may love in return? Bah! no—that can't be; and yet, somehow, there is a vacant corner in my old heart, and the image of that little girl seems to fill it exactly. I am an old fool, and yet—damn you, sir, what d'ye mean by running against me, eh!—and yet, it did me more good to see that hungry family last night, eat the food that I had provided for them, than it did when I, Gregory Grimsby, was promoted to the elevated rank of Corporal. Now about this little girl—I'll bet my three-cornered cock'd hat against a pinch of Scotch snuff that she has been abducted—entrapped into the power of some scoundrel for the worst of purposes. That's the most natural supposition that I can get at. Now display thy logic, Corporal: thy supposed scoundrel must be rich, for poor men can seldom afford such expensive luxuries as mistresses; being rich implies that he is *respectable*—so the world says and thinks—bah! Being respectable, he would not compromise his character by engaging personally in such a low business as entrapping a girl; no—he would employ an *agent*; and such an agent must necessarily be a very low person, whether male or female—if a male, he is a ruffian—if a female, she is a strumpet—and where do ruffians and strumpets, of the *lower orders* (for even in crime there is an aristocracy) [A] where do they usually reside? why, in a congenial atmosphere—in the lowest section of the city; and what is the lowest section of this city? why, *Ann street*, to be sure. Truly, Corporal Grimsby, thou art an admirable logician! So now I am on my way to Ann street, to explore its dens, in the hope (a vain one, I fear) of finding the supposed agent who was employed by the supposed rich scoundrel to abduct, kidnap, or entrap my little Fanny. Should I be so fortunate as to find that agent, money will readily induce him or her to divulge the place where the girl is hid; for the principle of "honor among thieves" has, I believe, but an imaginary existence."

> [A] The honest Corporal was right; the well-dressed, gentlemanly, speculating, wholesale swindler would scorn to associate with the needy wretch who protracts a miserable existence by small pilferings—and the fashionable courtezan who promenades Washington street and "sees company" at a splendidly furnished brothel, can perceive not the slightest resemblance between her position in society and that of the wretched troll who practises indiscriminate prostitution in some low "crib" in Ann street. And yet philosophy and common sense both level all moral distinction between the two conditions.—A noble murderer once protested against being hung on the same gallows with a chimney-sweep—there was aristocracy with a vengeance! We opine that the lofty and arrogant pretensions of some of our "nabobs," who are often of obscure and sometimes of ignominious birth, are scarcely less ridiculous than the aristocratic notions of a gentlemanly rascal who robs *a la mode* and picks a pocket with gentility and grace!

Leaving the Corporal to explore the intricate labyrinths of Ann street, (in the hope of obtaining some clew to the fate of Fanny Aubry,) thou wilt have the kindness, gentle reader, to accompany us into one of the squalid dens of that great sewer of vice and crime. But first we pause to read and admire the sign which decorates the exterior of a "crib" opposite Keith's Alley, and which, with a peculiarity of orthography truly amusing, notifies you that it is a *"Vittlin Sollor."* (This sign remains there to this day.) Passing on, we cannot fail to be impressed with the "mixed" nature of the society of the place; colored ladies and gentlemen (by far the most decent portion of the population) are every where to be seen, thronging the side-walks, indulging in boisterous laughter; loafers of every description are lounging about, whose tattered garments indicate the languishing condition of their wardrobes; great, ruffianly fellows stare at you with eyes expressive of the villainy that prompts to robbery and murder;—miserable men, ghastly women, and dirty children obstruct the pathway, and annoy you with their oaths and ribald jests. Let us descend this steep flight of steps, and enter this cellar. Be not too fastidious in regard to the odor of the place, for *eau de cologne* and otto of rose are not exactly the commodities disposed of here, the place being devoted to the sale of that beverage classically termed "rot-gut," and eatables which, unlike wine, are by no means improved in flavor by age. There is the "bar," and the red-nosed gentleman behind it seems to be one of its best patrons. A wooden bench extends around the apartment, and upon it are seated about twenty persons of both sexes. A brief sketch of a few of the "ladies" of this goodly company may prove interesting, from the fact that the names are real, and belong to prostitutes who even now inhabit the regions of Ann street.

That handsome, finely-formed female, with dark eyes and hair in ringlets, and who is also very neatly dressed, is "Kitty Cling-cling," who has been termed the "belle of Ann street." That lady in a red dress, with hair uncommonly short, (she having only recently dispensed with a wig,) is Joannah Westman, of Fleet street, and Liverpool Jane from the same *respectable* neighborhood. This renowned "Lady" of the town was (and is) distinguished by a huge scar on her left cheek, which seems to be the exact impression of a gin bottle, probably thrown in some brawl in Liverpool, her native place. Then there is Lize Whittaker, from Lowell, who "ties up" at the corner of Fleet and Ann streets. Then we notice two ladies who rejoice in the mellifluous names of "Bald-head" and "Cockroach," and who are both worthy representatives from Keith's Alley. These, with a small sprinkling of ebony lasses and their attendant cavaliers, make up the very respectable assemblage.

And now everybody brightens up, as a couple of colored gentlemen enter the cellar, and seating themselves upon a raised platform termed by courtesy "the orchestra," commence tuning a fiddle and base viol, preparatory to a dance by "all the characters."—Away the musicians glide into the harmonious measures of a gay quadrille—and to say the truth, the music is excellent, for Picayune and Joe are very skillful performers on their respective instruments; and are well qualified to play for a much more select and fashionable auditory. And now the voluptuous Kitty Cling-cling is led to the centre of the festive hall by a sable mariner, and begins to foot it merrily to the dulcet strains; while Bald-head and Cockroach find partners in two African geniuses, whose dress and general appearance would most decidedly exclude them from admission into a fancy ball at Brigham's. Away they go, through all the intricate mazes of the giddy dance. But see—a crowd of well-dressed but dissipated young men enter the cellar, their wild looks and disordered attire plainly indicating that they are on a regular "time." Those young men have been imbibing freely at some fashionable saloon in Court or Hanover street, and have come to consummate the evening's "fun" by having a dance with the fallen goddesses of Ann street. With a facetious perversity, they select as partners the most hideous of the negro women, and "mix in" the dance with a relish that could not be surpassed if their partners were each a Venus, and the cellar a magnificent hall of Terpsichore. The dance concluded, they throw down a handful of silver upon the counter, and invite "all hands to take a drink," but very rarely drink themselves in such a place, well knowing the liquor to be unworthy the palate of men accustomed to the superior beverages of the aristocratic establishments. At the completion of this ceremony, they take their departure, to visit some other "crib," and repeat the same performances.

But let us (supposing ourselves to be invisible) pass from the dance hall and enter the adjoining apartment, which is smaller. Seated around a rough deal table are about thirty men and women, engaged in smoking and drinking. The room is dimly lighted by a couple of tallow candles, stuck in bottles; the walls are black with dust and smoke, and the aforesaid table and a few benches constitute the entire furniture of the room. The general frequenters of the cellar are not admitted to this place, it being especially reserved for the use of those ladies and gentlemen who gain their living on the principle of an equal division of property—or in other words, *thieves*. In this room, secure from being overheard by the uninitiated and vulgar crowd, they could "ply the lush," and "blow a cloud," while they talked over their exploits and planned new depredations. The room was called the "Pig Pen," and the society who resorted there classed themselves under the expressive tide of "Grabbers." Although not a regularly organized association, it had a sort of leader or captain whose authority was generally recognized. This gentleman was called "Jew Mike," from the fact of his belonging to the Hebrew persuasion; he was a gigantic, swarthy ruffian, with a long, black and most repulsive features, and was dressed in a style decidedly "flash," his coat garnished with huge brass buttons, and his fingers profusely adorned with jewelry of the same material. He had recently graduated from the State Prison, where he had served a term of ten years for manslaughter, as the jury termed it; although it was universally regarded as one of the most cold-blooded and atrocious murders ever committed. To sum up the character of this man in a few words, he was a most desperate and bloodthirsty villain, capable of perpetrating the most enormous crimes; and dark hints were sometimes thrown out by his associates in reference to his former career; some said that he was an escaped murderer from the South; others that he had been a pirate; while all united in bearing unqualified testimony as to the villainy of his character and the number and blackness of his crimes. He could not plead *ignorance* in extenuation of his manifold enormities, for he possessed an education that would have qualified him to move in a respectable sphere of society, had he been so disposed. Upon his right was seated no less a personage that "Sow Nance," the hideous girl who had that day entrapped poor Fanny Aubry into the power of Mr. Tickels; she was much intoxicated, and by the maudlin fondness which she displayed for Jew Mike, it was easy to surmise the nature of the relation existing between her and him. Included in the company were several other "apple girls," whose proficiency as thieves entitled them to the distinction of being considered as competent "Grabbers;" each one of these wretched young creatures had her lover, of "fancy man," who was generally some low, petty thief—although, among the male portion of the assembly, there were several expert and daring robbers, the most distinguished of whom was Jew Mike himself, whose skill as a burglar had elevated him to the highly honorable position of captain of the "Grabbers."

The "lush" was freely handed round, and the company soon grew "half seas over;" then came wildly exaggerated narratives of exploits in robbery, thieving, and almost every species of crime, interspersed with smutty anecdotes and obscene songs, in which the females of the company were not a whit behind the males. At length Jew Mike himself was vociferously called on for either a song or a story; and not being a vocalist, the gentleman preferred entertaining his friends with the latter; so, clearing his throat by an enormous draught of brandy, he began as follows:

JEW MIKE'S STORY

"You see, lads and lasses, a year or two before I came to this accursed country to be *jugged for a ten spot*, for manslaughter, (it was a clear murder, though, and a good piece of work, too,) I was a nobleman's butler in the great city of London. Ah, *that* was the place for a man to get a living in! No decent

"Grabber," would stoop to petty stealing there; beautiful burglaries, yielding hundreds of pounds in silver plate; elegant highway robberies, producing piles of guineas and heaps of diamond watches,—that was the business followed by lads of the cross at that time in England. Well, there's no use in crying over spilt milk, any how; I was obliged to step out of England when the country got too hot to hold me, and if I returned there, by G——! my life wouldn't be worth a moment's purchase. And now to go on with my story. I was a nobleman's butler, and glorious times I had of it—little to do, plenty of pickings and stealings, free access to the pantry and wine-cellar, and enjoying terms of easy intimacy with the prettiest chambermaid in London. The only drawback upon my happiness was Lord Hawley's *valet*, a Frenchman, named Lagrange, who had been in his lordship's service many years, and was regarded as a remarkably honest and faithful man,—and so he was; but those qualities which rendered him valuable to his lordship, of course rendered him devilish obnoxious to me,—for he suspected my real character, and was continually playing the spy upon me, and informing my master of all my little peccadilloes. For instance, his lordship would send for me in his library, and say, sternly,—'Simpson, my valet Lagrange informs me that you are improperly intimate with one of the female domestics; you must stop it, or quit my service.' And perhaps the next day he would again summon me before him, and, with that cursed valet grinning maliciously at me from behind his chair, say to me,—'Simpson, I hear that you make too free with my wine, and are frequently intoxicated; stop it, or I shall dismiss you.' In short, Lagrange was the bane of my existence, and I secretly swore to be terribly revenged upon him for his tattling propensities. You'll soon see how well I kept my oath.

"My Lady Hawley was a very gay, dissipated and beautiful woman, and I had long been aware that during my master's absence she was in the habit of receiving the clandestine visits of a handsome young officer of dragoons. To tell the truth, I used to admit him to the house, and see that no one was in the way to observe him enter her ladyship's chamber, for which services I received very liberal rewards from both her ladyship, and Captain St. Clair. Lord Hawley doted upon his wife, who was many years younger than himself;

and often have I laughed in my sleeve when I thought what a cuckold she made of him. But he suspected nothing of the kind; I was the only person, besides the parties, who knew of the intrigue; even Lagrange, artful spy as he was, did not discover it. My master, who was addicted to gambling, was absent until a late hour every night, at Crockford's; and thus her ladyship had every opportunity to enjoy frequent interviews with her lover. As I knew of her frailty, I had her completely in my power; and often I was tempted to threaten her with exposure, unless she would "come down" handsomely with a thousand pounds or so, and grant me *any other favor* that I might choose to demand, as the price of my silence,—for, as I said before, she was a beautiful woman, and a butler has feelings as ardent as those of a captain of dragoons.

"Well, matters continued very quiet and agreeable, until late one night, after I had gone to bed, I heard a low but hurried knock at the door of my room. I arose, hastily threw on a few garments, and opened the door, when to my astonishment in rushed Lady Hawley, in her night-dress, and threw herself into a chair, breathless with agitation. Almost instantly the thought flashed through my mind that her intrigue had been discovered; cautiously closing the door, I advanced towards her ladyship, and in a respectful manner inquired why she had honored me with a visit so unexpected, and what might be the cause of her evident agitation, at the same time assuring her of my assistance, should she require it. She fixed her proud, beautiful eyes upon my face, and said, in a voice trembling with emotion,—

"'Good heavens, Simpson, only think of it, my foolish affair with Captain St. Clair is discovered!'

"'Is it possible, your ladyship?' I cried, 'and may I ask who—'

"'His lordship's valet, Lagrange, saw me, half an hour ago, conducting the Captain to the private stair-case which leads to the garden,' replied her ladyship, shuddering, and shading her face with her hands.

"'And might not your ladyship purchase his silence?' I asked. She replied,—

"'I have just come from his room; you know how obstinate he is,—how entirely devoted to his lordship,—how blindly honest and faithful he has ever been,—how singularly averse to receiving presents from any source whatever, fearing it might have the appearance of bribery. I went to his room, and offered him a hundred guineas if he would solemnly swear never to reveal what he had seen. In a tone of cold indifference he said, 'I must do my duty to his lordship, to whom I am bound by the strongest ties of gratitude, even at the sacrifice of your ladyship's honor.' I entreated him, almost on my knees, to give the required promise; I offered to double, nay, treble the sum that I had named, but no; he turned from me, almost with disdain, (the low-born menial!) and requested me to retire, as I must be aware of the impropriety of such a visit, at such an hour. Perceiving the uselessness of attempting to bribe him to secrecy, I left him, cursing him for his obstinacy, and came direct to you. Heavens!' added her ladyship, drawing her robe over her partially denuded bosom, 'how desperate the fear of exposure has made me, that in this indecent attire I go at midnight to the chambers of male servants!—Simpson, can you help me in this dreadful emergency? You have heretofore proved faithful to me,—do not desert me now. *Lagrange must be silenced!*—do you understand me? At any cost,—at any risk,—his babbling tongue must be hushed, *by you*, for you are the only person whom I can trust in the affair. Yes, he must never speak the word that will proclaim my dishonor to the world!'

"'*At any cost*, your ladyship?' rejoined I, fixing my eyes steadily upon hers, for her despair rendered me bold, and I was not one to suffer an opportunity to slip by unimproved.

"'I understand you, fellow!' she replied, with a hysterical laugh and a glance of scorn,—'and much as I despise you, I answer yes! at any cost. But, gracious Heavens, what do I say? *you*, a menial, a base-born servitor! But no matter; even *that* is far preferable to exposure. Good God! to think of being cast off by his lordship with loathing and contempt, despised and hated by my relatives,—an eternal blot upon my name,—forever excluded from the sphere of society of which I am the star and centre,—no, that shall never, never be. Silence Lagrange—silence him forever,—then ask of me any favor, and it shall not be denied.'

"I approached her ladyship; she was pale as marble, but how superbly beautiful! Her glossy hair, all disordered, hung in rich masses upon her uncovered shoulders; her seductive night-dress but imperfectly concealed the glories of her divine form,—her heaving bosom, so voluptuous and fair, was more than half disclosed to my gaze. With a palpitating heart I laid my trembling hand upon one of her plump, white shoulders. Never shall I forget the majestic rage and scorn of her look, as she started to her feet, and stood before me in all the pride of her imperial beauty.

"'Fellow,' she said, with desperate calmness, 'you are bold; but perhaps I ought to have expected this. I perceive that you are disposed to take every advantage of my situation. Be it so, then; but not until you have *earned the reward*, can you claim it. Remember this. Fortunately, his lordship is out of town, and will not return until the day after to-morrow; but oh! how unfortunate that his accursed valet did not accompany him! Lagrange pretended to be ill, and was left behind, and my lord was attended by another servant. No matter,—you will have an opportunity to dispose of this French spy ere the return of his master. I care not what method you take to silence his tongue,—but be secret and sure; and when the work is done, you shall have your reward—not before.'

"Having thus spoken, her ladyship swept out of the room with the air of a queen, leaving me to devise the best method of silencing Lagrange forever. I could not mistake her ladyship's meaning; she wished me to *murder* the man. Now, the fact is, ladies and gentlemen, murder's a devilish ticklish business, any how; not that I ever had any false delicacy in relation to the wickedness of the thing—pshaw! nothing of the kind,—you'll all believe me when I assure you that I'd as soon cut a human throat, as wring the neck of a chicken, for that matter; but then the consequences of a discovery are so ducedly unpleasant, and although I am confident in my own mind that I am destined to terminate my existence ornamented with a hempen cravat, I have never had any desire to hasten that consummation. So I didn't altogether relish the job which her ladyship had given me; but when I thought of her surpassing beauty, my hesitation vanished like mists before the rising sun, and I resolved to do it.

"Several times the next day I tried to provoke Lagrange into a quarrel, but the wily rascal, as if divining my intentions, only shrugged his shoulders and smiled in the cold and sarcastic manner peculiar to him. This enraged me greatly, and after applying the most abusive epithets to him, I finally struck him. But all availed nothing; unlike the majority of his countrymen, the fellow was cold and passionless, even under insults and blows. I had provided myself with a sharp butcher's knife, which I carried in my sleeve, ready to plunge into his heart, had he offered to attack me in return; and thus I hoped to make it appear that I had slain him in self-defence. But his admirable coolness and self-possession defeated that scheme,—and I saw that I would be obliged to slay him deliberately at the first opportunity.

"That opportunity was not long wanting.

"During the afternoon he had occasion to visit the wine vault, of which I alone had the key; I accompanied him thither, and while he was engaged in selecting some malt liquor for the servants' table, I said to him,—

"'Monsieur Lagrange, you are acquainted with a secret that intimately concerns her ladyship; what use do you intend to make of this knowledge?'

"The Frenchman very coolly intimated that it was none of my business, and continued his employment. His back was towards me; I approached nearer to him, and said, in a low tone—

"'You infernal, backbiting, sneaking scoundrel, you have often betrayed me to my master, and would now betray her ladyship. You shall not live to do it—die like a dog, as you are!'

"While thus addressing him, I had drawn forth my knife; and as I uttered the last words, I plunged it with all my force into his left side, up to the very handle. The blade passed directly through his heart, and without a groan he fell dead at my feet.

"No remorse—no sorrow for the bloody deed I had committed, found entrance to my soul; on the contrary, I gazed at the corpse with savage exultation. 'That babbling tongue is now forever hushed,' thought I; and then, as a sudden strange thought struck me, I added—'and that tongue shall be my passport to a bliss more exquisite than the joys of Paradise.' With an untrembling hand I cut off the dead man's tongue, secured it about me, and having hid the body behind a row of wine casks, left the cellar, securely locked the door, and then went about my usual avocations, resolving to dispose of the corpse that night in some manner that should avert suspicion from me, for I had every confidence in my own ingenuity.

"Towards evening, I sought and obtained an interview with her ladyship, in private. She advanced to meet me with a hurried step and sparkling eyes.

"'Simpson, *is it done*?' she asked, in a tone of extreme agitation, and laying her delicate hand on my arm.

"'It is, your ladyship,' was my reply, producing and holding before her the bloody evidence of the deed—'and here is the tongue of Lagrange,—the tongue that would have proclaimed your shame and effected your ruin, had its owner lived; but he now lies a cold corpse, and this once mischievous member is now as powerless as a piece of carrion beneath a butcher's shamble.'

"'And the body—how will you dispose of that?' she asked, shuddering, and turning from the sickening spectacle with disgust.

"'To-night it shall be sunk deep in the waters of the Thames,' I replied; and then, in a more familiar manner than I had as yet ventured to assume, I reminded her ladyship of the *reward* she had promised me, as soon as the job should be completed. Again she shuddered;—and turned deadly pale; and with a bitter smile, which seemed to me to be expressive of hatred and contempt combined, she answered—

"'You are right, Simpson; you have obeyed my wishes, and merit your reward,—but not now, not now! Come to my chamber at midnight; I shall expect you,—you understand. Go now—leave me; remove all traces of your crime. I shall take care to have a quantity of plate removed from the house to-night, and destroyed, and when his lordship returns to-morrow, he will imagine that Lagrange, despite his supposed faithfulness and integrity, has absconded and stolen the plate,—that will account to him for the valet's sudden disappearance. Leave me.'

"'Remember, at midnight, your ladyship,' said I, and left her; but when I had closed the door of the apartment, I imagined that I heard her give utterance to a scornful laugh.

However, I attributed it to her gratification at the death of Lagrange, and descending to the wine cellar, I busied myself in washing away the stains of blood from the floor. How impatiently I longed for the arrival of midnight! the hour that was to bring with it the reward of my crime!

"During the evening, I paid a visit to a noted *"boozing ken"* in St. Giles', which bore the very suitable appellation of the "Jolly Thieves." Here I engaged two desperate fellows of my acquaintance—(for I went on a *crack*, now and then, myself, just to keep my hand in,)—to make away with the body of Lagrange; they were to come to the rear of my master's house, an hour after midnight, provided with a sack and some means of conveyance; and, for a liberal reward, they promised to carry off the corpse, and, having attached a heavy weight to it, sink it in the Thames,—although I felt assured in my own mind, that, instead of giving it to the fishes, they would make a more profitable disposition of it, by selling it to some surgeon for dissection;—body-snatching being a part of their profession, as well as burglary and murder. Having made this important arrangement, and paid them a good round sum in advance, (for I was well provided with money,) I returned to my master's house, which I reached about eleven o'clock.

"At length the welcome midnight hour arrived, and with a beating heart I repaired to the chamber of her ladyship. It was a large apartment, furnished with exquisite taste and elegance,—in fact, a perfect bower of the graces; and, to my somewhat voluptuous mind, not the least attractive feature of it, was a magnificent and luxurious *bed*, mysteriously hidden beneath a profuse cloud of snowy drapery, heavily laden with costly lace. I had already pictured to myself the delights of an amorous dalliance within that bower of Venus, with one whose glorious beauty could not have been surpassed by that of the ardent goddess herself—but how grievously was I doomed to be disappointed, at the very moment when I fancied my triumph certain! But I must not anticipate my story.

"In answer to my respectful, and I must own, somewhat timid, knock at the chamber door, I heard the musical but subdued voice of her ladyship bidding me to 'come in.' I entered, and having softly closed the door, noiselessly turned the key in the lock, and advanced to where she was seated by a table, upon which there stood wine, and materials of a *recherche* supper. Drawing a chair close to her ladyship, I seated myself, and gazed at her long and ardently, while she, apparently unconscious of my presence, seemed to be deeply engaged in perusing a splendid volume of Byron's poems.

"Surprised and not perfectly at ease, in consequence of her silence and abstraction (for she had not even glanced at me,) I at length ventured to observe—

"'Your ladyship sees that I am punctual; as of course I could not neglect to keep so delightful an appointment.'

"Still she answered nothing, nor even raised her eyes from the book! During the silence of some minutes that ensued, I had an excellent opportunity to feast my eyes upon the seraphic loveliness of her face, and the admirable proportions of her queen-like form. She was dressed with studied simplicity, and in a style half *neglige*, infinitely more fascinating than the most elaborate full dress. A robe of snowy whiteness, made so as to display her plump, soft arms, and fine, sloping shoulders, and entirely without ornament, constituted her attire; and a single white rose alone relieved the jet darkness of her clustering hair. She was seated in a manner that enabled me to view her profile to the best advantage; I was never more forcibly struck with its purely classical and Grecian outlines; and I observed that a soft expression of melancholy was blended with the usual *hauteur* that sat enthroned upon her angelic features.

"As I gazed admiringly upon the beautiful woman, whom I could almost imagine to be a being from a celestial world, I could not help saying to myself—

"'After all, she is an adulteress and a murderess; and is now about to sacrifice her person to me, the instrument of her murderous wishes. Why, what a devil is here, in the form of a lovely woman, whose beauty would seem to proclaim her a tenant of the skies, while the black depravity of her heart fits her only for the companionship of the fiends below! Why do I hesitate and tremble in her presence? She is in my power—my *slave*! Yet, by heavens, what a superb creature! A thousand passionate devils are dancing in her brilliant eyes—her lips are moist with the honey of love—and her form seems to glow with ardent but hidden fires! Come, let me delay no longer, but speak to her in the language befitting a master to his slave!'

"'Lady,' said I, in a tone familiar, yet not disrespectful—'why this reserve and silence? You know for what purpose I come thus at midnight to your chamber—it is by your own appointment, and to receive the reward of a difficult and dangerous service which I have performed for you. Nay, I see that you have anticipated my coming, by preparing this delicate and acceptable feast for our entertainment. Is it not so, my charmer? And you have dressed yourself in this bewitching style of chaste simplicity, solely to please me—am I right? But come; though you have not yet spoken or looked at me, sweet coquette that you are, I read in your bright eyes the confirmation of my hopes. Let us first banquet upon the delights of love, and then sip the ruby contents of the sparkling wine-cup, which I'll swear are not one half so sweet as the nectar of your lips, which now I taste.'

"I clasped her in my arms as I spoke, and attempted to imprint a kiss upon her lips; but she hurled me from her with disdain, and said, with an air of lofty dignity—

"'Dog, how dare you thus intrude into the sanctity of my chamber? and how dared you for a moment presume to think that I intended to keep the promise which, in my eagerness to have Lagrange silenced, I gave you? Know that, sooner than submit to your base and loathsome embraces, I'd brave exposure and even death itself! If *money* will satisfy you, name your sum, and be it ever so great, it shall be paid to you; but presume not to think that Lady Adelaide Hawley can ever so far forget her birth and rank, as to debase herself with such as you.'

"'*Money*, your ladyship, was not what I bargained for,' I boldly replied; for the scorn and contempt with which she treated me, stung me to the quick, and enraged me beyond all measure. 'If your ladyship refuses to perform, honorably and fairly, your part of the contract, you must take the consequences; you shall be proclaimed as an adulteress, and as an accessory to the crime of murder.'

"'Fool!' she cried—yet her countenance indicated the fear she really felt, notwithstanding the boldness of her words—'fool! expose me at your peril! You dare not, for your own neck would be stretched in payment for your treachery, while your charges against me, low, miserable menial that you are, would never be believed—never! Such accusations against me, a peeress of the realm, and a lady whose reputation has never been assailed, would but add to the general belief in your own guilt, and the certainty of your fate; such charges would be regarded as a paltry subterfuge, and no one would credit them. Go, fellow—the bat cannot consort with the eagle, nor can such as you aspire to even the most distant familiarity with persons of my rank. Depart, instantly; and to-morrow you shall receive a pecuniary reward that will amply compensate you for the disappointment you now feel.'

"With these words she turned away from me, waving her hand in token that the conference was closed; but I was enraged and desperate, as much by the scorn of her manner as by the disappointment I felt. A hell of passion was burning in my heart; and I said to her, in a low, deep tone—

"'Woman, you shall be mine, even if I am obliged to commit another murder—I swear it! I hesitated not at perpetrating a deed of blood; nor will I hesitate now to obtain, by violence and even bloodshed, the reward you promised me for that deed! Lady, be wise; we are alone at this silent hour—I am powerful and you are helpless. Consent, then, or—'

"She interrupted me with a scornful laugh, that rendered me almost frantic with fury. Reason forsook me; I lost all self-control, and rushed upon her with the ferocity of a madman, determined to strangle her.

"Ere I could lay my grasp upon her, I was seized with a force that nearly stunned me. I arose with difficulty, and to my astonishment beheld the handsome countenance and glittering uniform of her ladyship's favored lover, Captain St. Clair!

"'Villain,' said he, in his usual cold and haughty manner, (he was of noble blood, and as proud as Lucifer,) 'you little imagined that I was a witness of the entire scene in which you have played so praiseworthy a part! Upon my honor, you are the most ambitious of butlers! Cooks and chambermaids are not sufficiently delicate for your fastidious taste, forsooth!— but you must aspire to ladies of noble birth! Faith, I should not be surprised to hear of your attempting an intrigue with her gracious Majesty, the Queen! Hark'ee, fellow, begone! and thank my moderation that I do not punish you upon the spot, for your infernal presumption! Yet I would scorn to tarnish the lustre of my good sword with the blood of such a thing as thou!'

"'Captain,' said I, boldly, (for I am no coward, ladies and gentlemen, as you all know,) 'as you have seen fit to play the spy, it is fair to presume that you are acquainted with the circumstances upon which my claim to the favor of this lady is based. At her instigation, and prompted by her promises of reward, I have murdered Lord Hawley's valet, Lagrange, in order to prevent his revealing to his master, the criminal intimacy existing between you and her ladyship. Now, Captain, I submit it to you as a man of honor—having committed such a deed, and exposed myself to such a fearful risk, am I not entitled to the reward promised by her ladyship? without the hope of which reward, I never would have bedewed my hands in the blood of my fellow servant. And can I justly be blamed for claiming that reward, and even for attempting to obtain it by force, since I have faithfully earned it?'

"The Captain laughed, half in good nature, half in scorn, and said—

"'Faith, you are a well-spoken knave, and appeal to my honor as if you were my equal; and I am half inclined to pardon your presumption on account of your wit. Now listen, my good fellow;—her ladyship, as a measure of policy, wished to have a certain person removed, who was possessed of a dangerous secret; now you were the only available agent she could employ to effect that removal. But you demanded a certain favor, (which shall be nameless,) as the price of your services, and would accept of no other remuneration. The danger was imminent; what could her ladyship do? The man must be disposed of, even at the sacrifice of truth; her ladyship gave the required promise (*intending never to keep it*,) you performed the service, and very properly, I own, come to receive your reward. Of course, you perceive the impossibility of a compliance with your wishes. No intrigue can exist between the patrician and the plebeian—you are low-born, she of the noblest blood of the kingdom. Are you so blind, man, that you cannot see—or are you so stupid that you cannot comprehend—the repugnance which her ladyship must naturally feel at the very idea of an amorous intimacy existing between a high-born lady and—good heavens!—a *butler*? Here, my good fellow, is a purse, containing fifty guineas—I will double the sum tomorrow. Now go; and remember that you have everything to expect from our generosity, in a pecuniary point of view; but a repetition of your demand for her ladyship's favors, will most assuredly result to your lasting disadvantage.'

"Seeing the folly of attempting to press my claim further, I sneaked out of the room, with very much the air of a disconcerted cur with his tail between his legs, to use a simile more expressive than elegant. The moment I had entered my own chamber, the clock in a neighboring steeple proclaimed the hour of two, and then for the first time I remembered the appointment which I had made with my two particular friends, from the "Jolly Thieves," in reference to the disposal of Lagrange's body. The hour appointed for meeting them, was passed; and suddenly a thought struck me—a strange thought—which had no sooner flashed through my mind, than I resolved to act upon its suggestion. 'Twas a glorious plan of revenge, and one which could only have emanated from my fertile imagination.

"'The corpse of the Frenchman shall become the instrument of my vengeance,' thought I, chuckling with glee. 'I shall not need the assistance of those two fellows now—and, if they are still lurking about the house, I will reward them for their trouble and send them away. Ah, lucky thought—lucky thought!'

"I found my two friends in waiting for me; they grumbled much at my want of punctuality, but their murmurings were hushed when I paid them liberally, and dismissed them, saying that I had discovered a much safer and more convenient method of disposing of the body, than the plan originally proposed, and therefore should not require their assistance.—They departed, rejoicing at their good fortune in being freed from a difficult and dangerous task, and congratulating themselves on having received as much money as they had been promised for its performance.

"Taking with me a dark lantern, I descended noiselessly into the wine vault, and having secured the massive iron door, proceeded to execute my plan of vengeance. Comrades, can you guess what that plan was? No, I'll swear you cannot. But listen, and you shall hear.

"Placing my light in a convenient position, I dragged the dead body of Lagrange from its place of concealment; then I bent over it, and examined the ghastly countenance. The features were pale and rigid, the teeth firmly set, and the glassy eyes wide open and staring. The awful expression of those dead orbs seemed, bold as I was, to freeze my very soul as with the power of a basilisk. For a single moment I repented the deed; but that feeling soon passed, and I rejoiced at it.

"It occurred to me to search the pockets of my victim; I did so, and found a small sum of money, and a sealed letter, addressed to Lord Hawley. The valet had probably intended to despatch that letter to his master that afternoon—which design was frustrated by his sudden death by my hand. Eagerly I broke the seal, and read as follows:—

"'LONDON.

"'My lord.—Should your lordship have possibly designed extending your visit to Berkshire beyond the time originally allotted to the same, I entreat your lordship to set aside every consideration—every engagement, however pressing or important its nature may be, and to return immediately to town. Something has occurred, in the conduct of her ladyship, intimately affecting your lordship's honor. To relieve your lordship from any painful uncertainty that may be occasioned by this indefinite announcement, you will pardon me for stating plainly, that I myself saw her ladyship and Captain St. Clair, under circumstances that admitted of but one opinion in reference to the nature of the intimacy existing between them. Simpson, the butler, whom I am persuaded is in the confidence of her ladyship and the Captain, this afternoon questioned me in regard to my knowledge of the affair, and the use I intended to make of that knowledge; and he, not deeming my replies satisfactory, abused and struck me. My duty to your lordship prevented any retaliation on my part; and that duty, (the offspring of humble gratitude for your lordship's many acts of generous kindness to me, both in this country and in France,) now impels me to communicate these unpleasant facts—which I do, with sincere sorrow for her ladyship's indiscretion, and every desire for the preservation of your lordship's honor.

"'From your lordship's humble servant,
"'LOUIS LAGRANGE.'

"This letter, so characteristic of the polished, wily and educated Frenchman, was written in the French language, with which I was well acquainted, I therefore easily translated it. After a careful perusal, I placed it in my pocket-book—for I was well aware that it might one day prove a valuable auxiliary to me, should I feel disposed to inform my master of his wife's infidelity, and his lordship then could not doubt the truth of his own favorite and faithful servant, in whom he had the most unbounded confidence.

"'Oh, scornful Lady Hawley and sarcastic Captain St. Clair!' I could not forbear exclaiming—'ye shall both be caught in a net of your own making, when ye least expect it! My lady will be turned out of doors as an adulteress; and my gentleman will perhaps be shot through the head by the husband he has wronged! Patience, patience, good Simpson; thou shalt yet riot in the very satiety of thy vengeance. But now to put in operation my first method—an ingenious one it is, too—of avenging my wrongs!'

"Among the various wines with which the extensive cellar was abundantly stocked, was a large cask containing a particular kind, of a very rich and peculiar flavor; and of this wine I knew Lady Hawley, who was a luxurious woman, very fastidious in her taste, to be especially fond. Captain St. Clair, too, preferred it above all other kinds; and at the midnight suppers which he so often enjoyed with her ladyship, the ruby contents of this particular cask was most frequently called into requisition, as I well know, for I had been accustomed to carry it from the cellar to the door of the bed-chamber wherein the amorous pair indulged in the joys both of Venus and of Bacchus. The wine had been imported by his lordship, who was a *bon vivant*, from Bordeaux and was particularly valued for its rich color, solid body, and substantial yet delicate flavor, rivalling in these qualities, perhaps, that classic beverage, the famed Greek wine.

"'I will add to the exquisite flavor of this wine,' said I—'her ladyship and her lover shall banquet on human blood; the corruption of a putrifying corpse shall be mingled with the sparkling fluid that nourishes their unholy passions.'

"With but little difficulty, and less noise, (for I well understood such matters,) I removed the head of the cask, which I found to be about half full. How luxurious was the odor that arose from the dark liquid, fragrant with spices! Taking a small vessel, I drank a bumper—then another. My blood instantly became charged with a thousand fires; my heart seemed to swell with mighty exultation; my brain seemed to swim in a sea of delight. I laughed with mad glee to think of the superb vengeance I was about to wreak on my enemies; then I raised the corpse of Lagrange with Herculean strength, thrust it into the cask, and pressed it into the smallest possible compass; but found to my inexpressible chagrin, that it would be absolutely impossible to re-adjust the head of the cask, unless the body was in some manner made smaller. After a few moments' reflection, a happy thought struck me. I hesitated not a moment, but drew a sharp clasp knife from my pocket, deliberately severed the head from the body, and thrust it into the cask. Then, without the least difficulty, I replaced the top of the cask, and my work was accomplished.

"I repaired to my chamber but slept not, as you may suppose; the events of that day and night had been of a nature too singularly exciting to admit of repose. Shortly after I had retired, I heard Lady Hawley conduct her lover to the back stair-case; there was a sound of kissing, and a whispered appointment made for another meeting, on a night when his lordship would probably be absent. 'Yes, and at that interview, my amorous pair,' thought I, 'shall you taste of the wine which I have improved by an addition which you little suspect, but with which you shall one day be made acquainted.' And then I laughed till the tears rolled down my cheeks.

"Lord Hawley returned at the expected time, and immediately inquired for his valet, Lagrange. The gentleman was, of course, among the missing; and I overheard her ladyship announcing to her husband that the Frenchman had absconded, carrying off plate and jewelry to a considerable amount. Lord Hawley was extremely shocked and grieved on receiving this (false) intelligence; and I heard him mutter, as he retired in great perturbation of mind to his study,— 'What, can it be possible?—Lagrange, whom I esteemed to be the most honest and faithful fellow in the world—of whose fidelity I have had so many evidences,—whom I have often benefitted,—can it be that *he* has deserted and robbed me? Then indeed do I believe all mankind to be false as hell!'

"A week passed, and nothing occurred in Hawley House worthy of mention. At the expiration of that time, his lordship went on a short journey, (connected with some political object,) which would occasion him a fortnight's absence from home. Then was her ladyship and the captain in clover! and then was afforded me an opportunity to set before them the wine which I had enriched by my famous *addition*!

"Not deeming it necessary to adopt the usual precautions, my lady feasted, toyed and dallied with her handsome lover in her own private apartments, fearing no detection, as she was certain that her husband would not return before the specified time, and as I was the only person aware of the captain's presence in the house; she feared not, thinking that I dared not betray her, as she imagined that I was completely in her power on account of the murder I had committed. Pretty fool! she little thought of the plan I had formed for her destruction, and that of her haughty and hated paramour.

"I waited on them at table in my humblest and most respectful manner; and I could perceive that they inwardly congratulated themselves on having, as they thought, completely subdued me, and bribed me to eternal silence with regard to their amours.

"At their very first banquet, (for the splendor of their repasts merited that high-sounding title,) I was requested to bring from the cellar a decanter of their *favorite* wine. You may be sure I did not mistake the cask, comrades. I drew from the cask which contained the corpse of Lagrange, a quantity of the wine, and holding it to the light, observed with intense satisfaction that it had assumed a darker tinge—it looked just like blood. For a moment I was tempted to *taste* it; but damn me! bad and blood-thirsty as I was, I could not do *that*. The corpse had been soaking in the wine a full week; I was convinced that the liquid was pretty thoroughly impregnated with the flavor of my scientific improvement; and even my stomach revolted at the idea of drinking wine tainted and reeking with the dead flesh and blood of the man I had murdered.

"I placed the wine on the table before my lady and the Captain; and I am free to confess that I trembled somewhat, in view of the possibility of their detecting, at the first taste, the trick which I had played them. Very nervous was I, when the Captain slowly poured out a wine glass full, and raised it to his lips; but how delighted was I, when he drained every drop of it with evident satisfaction, smacked his lips, and said to the lady—

"'By my faith, Adelaide, 'tis a drink for the gods! How that wine improves by age! Never before has it tasted so rich, so fruity, so delicious! Observe what a firm body it has—what deep, rich color—a fitting hue for a soldier's beverage, for 'tis red as blood. Allow me to fill your ladyship's glass, that you may judge of its improved and wonderful merits.'

"Her ladyship drank, and pronounced it excellent. I was in silent extacies. 'Drink the blood and essence of the murdered dead, ye fools, and call it sweet as honey to your taste!' I mentally said—'ere many days your souls shall be made sick with the knowledge of *what* ye have drank!'

"The guilty pair were not in the slightest degree reserved in my presence; on the contrary they jested, they talked, they indulged in familiarities before my face, in a manner that astonished me not a little. Comrades, none of you have seen much of fashionable life, I take it; for although you all belong to the very best society in Ann street, you can't reasonably be supposed to have much of an idea of society as 'tis seen in the mansion of an English nobleman. Therefore, if you don't think my yarn already too tedious, (it's as true as gospel, every word of it, upon the unsullied honor of a gentleman!) and if you'd like to know something of the capers of rich and fashionable people in high life, I'll tell you, in as few words as possible, some of the sayings and doings of my lady Hawley and her handsome lover, Captain St. Clair, as witnessed by me, at the time of which I have been speaking, in London."

Jew Mike paused to take breath and "wet his whistle;" while all his listeners eagerly requested him to "go on" with his yarn. During the progress of the narrative, an old, comical looking man, not over well dressed, had entered the room, unnoticed; and seating himself in one corner, he pulled a pipe from his pocket, lighted it, and began to smoke, at the same time taking a keen and intelligent survey of the motley assembly. Jew Mike, having quenched his thirst, resumed his story. [The reader will be good enough to observe, that while we give the substance of this worthy gentleman's narrative, we pretend not to give his precise words. It is highly probable that he adapted his language to the humble capacities of his low and illiterate auditors; and we have taken the liberty to clothe his ideas in words better suited to the more intelligent and refined understandings of our readers.]

"Well, ladies and gentlemen," said Jew Mike—"as I was saying, Lady Hawley and Captain St. Clair got so bad that they never minded my presence a bit, but talked and acted before me with as much freedom as if I were both deaf and blind. My lady would dress herself in the Captain's uniform, which fitted her to a charm, for she was a large, magnificent woman, while he was of no great stature for a man, although exceedingly well-made and handsome. Not was that all: the Captain would attire himself in her splendid garments, and, but for his moustache and imperial, might have passed for a very handsome woman. And, to carry out the idea still further, my lady would pretend to take very wild and improper liberties with her lover, which he would affect to resent with all the indignation proper to his assumed sex. Then they would roll and tumble upon the soft carpet until they were quite spent and breathless; after which the Captain would run into the chamber, and conceal himself beneath, behind, or *in* the bed; she would follow in pursuit, close the chamber door, and—I would apply my eye to the key-hole; but as I am a polite man, and as there are ladies present, (ahem!) you'll excuse me for not entering into particulars.

"So much for their actions, now for their words. I was attending them at supper one night, and to say the truth they were both of them highly elevated in consequence of having too profusely imbibed their favorite wine, seasoned with the *essence of Lagrange,* the name which I had privately given it. The Captain was very slightly attired, and my lady had on nothing but a very *intimate* garment, which revealed rather more than it concealed—for they had just before been playing the very interesting game of "hide and seek," and had not yet resumed all their appropriate garments. I had formerly regarded lady Hawley as the very *beau ideal* of all that was dignified, haughty and majestic; but that night she looked lewd and sensual, in an eminent degree, and appeared utterly reckless of all decency. She exposed her person in a manner that astonished me, and seemed to abandon herself without reserve, to all the promptings of her voluptuous nature. Her appearance, conversation and actions were not without their influence on me, you may be sure; and if ever I envied mortal man, it was that young officer, who could revel at will in the arms of the beautiful wanton at his side.

"The Captain, reclining his head upon her fair bosom, said—

"'And so Adelaide, in a few days your odious husband will return, and terminate these rapturous blisses. Why in the devil's name don't the accursed old man die of apoplexy, or break his neck, or get shot in a duel, or do something to relieve us of his hated interference with our stolen joys?'

"'Ah, St. Clair,' answered the lady, with a glance of passion— 'would that the old man were dead! Since I have tasted the sweets of your society—since I first listened to the music of your voice, and since first this heart beat tumultuously against yours, my whole nature is changed—my blood is turned to fire; my religion is my love for you; my deity is your image, and my heaven—is in your arms. Oh,' she suddenly exclaimed, as the rich blood mantled on her face and neck—'how terrible it is for a young and passionate woman to be linked in marriage to an old, impotent, cold, passionless being, who claims the name of *man*, but is not entitled to it! And then if she solaces herself with a lover— as she must, or die—she is continually agitated with fears of her husband's jealousy, and the dread of discovery. Like the thirsty traveller in a barren waste, her soul yearns for an ocean of delights—and pants and longs in vain. Husband— would that there was no such word, no such relation as it implies—'tis slavery, 'tis madness, to be chained for life to but one source of love, when a thousand streams would not satiate or overflow. Yet the world—the world—disgraces and condemns such as I am, if discovered; it points to my withered husband, and says—'there is your only *lawful* love.' Heavens! the very thought of him sickens and disgusts me; *he* a lover! He is no more to be compared to thee, my St. Clair, than is the withered leaf of autumn to the ripe peach or juicy pomegranate!'

"'By all the gods of war,' exclaimed the Captain, fired with admiration at her beauty and the fervor of her passion for him, and straining her to his breast in a perfect phrenzy of transport—'thy husband shall be no longer a stumbling-block between us, angel of my soul; I will insult him—he will challenge me—we will fight—I am the best shot in Europe, and he will be shot through the heart, if the cold dotard have one. Yet stay—damn it, why not have him disposed of after the manner of the valet? Ha, ha! a good thought! Simpson, what say you? Will you do it for a couple of hundred guineas, and without laying claim to the favors of her ladyship?'

"The last sentence was uttered with a very palpable sneer; it enraged me, for by it I was reminded of the manner in which I had been swindled out of the reward promised for my other murder. Besides, the man's cool villainy, and the woman's shameless lechery, disgusted me, bad as I was; for they belonged to that class which professes all the gentility, refinement and virtue in the world; and to hear the one glorying in adultery, and the other deliberately proposing murder, afforded such a damnable instance of the sublime hypocrisy peculiar to the "upper ten" of society, that I became desperately angry, and answered the Captain in a manner that astonished him.—You will remember, comrades, that as great a villain as I am, I am no hypocrite, and was never accused of being one. And yet hypocrisy prevails in every department of life. Look," continued Jew Mike, getting into a philosophical strain, and stroking his enormous beard with an air of profound complacency—"Look at that venerable looking old gentleman, who every Sabbath stands in his pulpit to declaim against wickedness and fleshy lusts. Mark his libidinous eye, as he follows that painted strumpet to her filthy den. There's hypocrisy. Then turn your eyes toward a sister city, and mark that grey-headed, sanctimonious editor, who every week solemnly prates of honesty, sobriety, and their kindred virtues. 'What an excellent man he is,' exclaim the whole tribe of fat, tea-drinking old women in mob-caps, raising their pious eyes and snuffy noses to heaven.—Ha, ha, ha! Why, ladies and gentlemen, that editor is so cursedly dishonest and so im—*mensely* mean, that his hair wouldn't stay black, but turned to a dirty white before its time—so mean, his food won't digest easy—his shirt won't dry when washed—his clothes won't fit him—the cholera won't have him—musquitoes won't bite him—and if, after his lean carcass is huddled under the turf, his cunning little soul should attempt to crawl through the key-hole of hell's gate, the devil, whose lacky he has ever been, would kick him with as much disgust as this *fraction* once displayed in kicking a poor wretch whom he had beggared, starved and ruined!

"But I see, comrades, that you begin to grow impatient at this moralizing—and well you may, for 'tis always distasteful to look at such reptiles as we have been contemplating. Well, to take up the thread of my yarn, which I shall bring to a close as speedily as possible, for 'tis getting late.—When the Captain proposed that I should murder Lord Hawley, his and her ladyship's hypocrisy enraged me to such an extent, that I boldly looked him in the face, and said to him—

"'Say, who is the greater villain, you or I? You, who prate of your birth, rank and position in life, and propose a murder, or I, making no pretensions whatever, I that have committed a murder at the instigation of one of your class, in the hope of reward? Look you, Captain; neither you nor your noble strumpet at your side shall bribe me to commit further crime. Wretches that you both are, false in honor and in truth, know that I am already fearfully revenged upon you—and your exposure is at hand. Another murder, indeed!—*have you not both drank blood enough?*'

"This last sentence I uttered with such significance that the Captain started and turned pale. 'What mean you, scoundrel?' he demanded.

"'Follow me, both of you, to the wine cellar!' I exclaimed in answer, fully determined to reveal the awful truth to them at once. Astonished and subdued by the impressiveness of my manner and the singularity of my words, they obeyed. Having seized a light from the table, I led the way to the cellar, and advanced to the cask wherein rotted the remains of the murdered Lagrange.

"The scene must have been a striking one, comrades. There was the vast vault, dimly lighted by a single wax taper; around were many black and mouldering casks containing the juice of the grape, some of which was of a great age. Before one of those casks, much larger than the others, stood I, brandishing aloft the implement with which I was about to break open that strange tomb, and disclose its awful secret. Beside me, dressed in the slight garments I have already described, their pale countenances expressive of mingled curiosity and fear, stood Lady Hawley and Captain St. Clair, whom I thus addressed—

"'This cask, may it please your ladyship and the Captain, contains the wine which you both are so extremely fond of. You have observed, with some surprise, that its flavor has of late much improved. I shall now, with your permission, show you the cause of that improvement, for which—ha, ha, ha!—you are solely indebted to me. The opening of this cask will disclose a mystery that you have never dreamed of. Look!'

"They both strained forward in eager expectation. A few blows sufficed to remove the head of the cask. Horror! a sickening stench arose, and there became visible the headless trunk of a human being. That portion of the body which was not immersed in the wine, was putrid. 'Look here!' cried I, in mad triumph, plunging my arm into the cask, and drawing forth the ghastly head of Lagrange. I held aloft the horrid trophy of my vengeance; there were the dull, staring eyes, the distorted features, and drops of wine oozed from between the set teeth. With a long, loud shriek, her ladyship fell to the ground insensible; muttering fierce curses on me, the Captain turned to raise her, and profiting by the opportunity, I escaped from the cellar and fled from the house. Making the best of my way to the 'Jolly Thieves,' in St. Giles, I sought safety and concealment there, where I had ample leisure to mature my future plans.

"In a day or two I saw it announced in one of the newspapers that a cask had been found floating in the river Thames, which on opening was found to contain the body and head of a man, and a quantity of wine. The circumstance gave rise to the supposition that the body had been procured by some surgeon for dissection, and for some reason had been abandoned and thrown overboard. The cask and its contents had, of course, been thrown into the river through the agency of the Captain; and the affair gave rise to neither excitement nor investigation.

"Meanwhile, Lord Hawley had returned to town. No sooner was I apprised of the fact, than I sent him the following blunt and somewhat rude epistle—for I felt too keen a thirst for vengeance on my enemies to admit of my being very choice or respectful in my language, even to a nobleman:—

"'My lord,—you are a cuckold. Do you doubt it? I can prove it, beyond the shadow of a doubt. Captain Eugene St. Clair is your lady's lover—she is his mistress. For a long time past, she has, during your absence, received him into her chamber. You are laughed at by the pretty pair, as a withered, impotent old dotard. You know the handwriting of your late valet, Lagrange. Accompanying this is a letter written by him, to you; before he had an opportunity of sending it to you, he was *made away with*, through the instrumentality of your amiable wife, who had every reason to suppose that he would betray her. The tale trumped up by the noble harlot about the Frenchman's having stolen your property and fled, is a lie. My lord, I think you have reason to be grateful to me for exposing the guilty parties; if so, any pecuniary reward which you may see fit to send me, by one of your servants, (I am at the *Jolly Thieves*, in St. Giles,) will be gratefully accepted by

MICHAEL SIMPSON.'

"I thus freely disclosed my place of concealment to his lordship, because I apprehended no danger to myself, knowing that the nobleman was a man of honor, who would not injure the person who had rendered him such an important service as to put him on the track to avenge his wrongs. And I also anticipated receiving a liberal reward for my information; nor was I disappointed,—for that very evening a servant in the Hawley livery called at the *Jolly Thieves*, and presented me with a small package, which on opening I found to contain bank notes to the amount of five hundred pounds, and the following note, which though in his lordship's handwriting, bore neither address nor signature:—

"'Here is the reward of your information. Accept, also, my thanks. The proof you have furnished of the truth of your statement, admits of no doubt. I know how to punish the w**e and her blackguard paramour. You had better leave the country, for I can surmise what agency *you* had in the affair of Lagrange's disappearance; but as you were the tool of others, I stoop not to molest you. Should the event, however, gain notoriety, *the law* of course, will not prove equally considerate.'

"I was overjoyed! Five hundred pounds, and the certainty of having ruined my enemies! That night I gave a sumptuous supper to all the frequenters of the *Jolly Thieves*; and a jolly time we had of it, I'll assure you, comrades. The most respectable men in London were present at the feast; there were nine cracksmen, five highwaymen, twelve pickpockets, two murderers, three gentlemen who had escaped from transportation, and a smart sprinkling of small workmen, in the way of *fogle hunters*, (handkerchief thieves,) and *body snatchers*, (grave robbers). Full forty of us sat down to a smoking supper of stewed tripe and onions,—ah, how my mouth waters to think of it now! And then the *lush!*—gallons of ale, rivers of porter, and oceans of grog! Every gentleman present volunteered a song; and when it came to be my turn, I gave the following, which, (being something of a poet,) I had myself composed, expressly for the occasion, to the air of the *Brave Old Oak*:—

SONG OF THE JOLLY THIEF

"A song to the thief, the jolly, jolly thief,
Who has plied his trade so long;—
May he ne'er come down to the judge's frown,
Or the cells of Newgate strong.
'Tis a noble trade, where a living's made
By an art so bold and free;
May he never be snug in a cold, stone jug,
Or swing from a two-trunk'd tree!

CHORUS
Then here's to the thief, the jolly thief
Who plies his trade so bold—
May he never see a turnkey's key,
Or sleep in a prison cold!

"This song was received with the most uproarious applause by the jovial crew; and we separated at a late hour, after giving three groans for the new police.

"A few days passed away. I never neglected each morning to carefully peruse all the newspapers; and just as I was beginning to despair of ever seeing any announcement calculated to assure me that my enemies were overthrown, I had the intense satisfaction of reading the following paragraph in the *Times*:—

"'AN AFFAIR OF HONOR. Yesterday morning, his lordship Viscount Hawley and the Honorable Captain Eugene

St. Clair had a hostile meeting in the suburbs of London. Circumstances of a delicate nature, of which we are not at liberty to speak at present, are reported to have led to the difficulty between the noble gentlemen. At the first fire Captain St. Clair fell, and upon examination it was found that he had been shot through the heart. He died instantly. His lordship was uninjured, and immediately departed for the Continent unaccompanied by her ladyship.'

"I danced with delight when I read this paragraph. 'My vengeance is already half accomplished,' thought I. But what had become of Lady Hawley? The newspapers, from day to day and from week to week, were silent with respect to her fate. At length I began to fear that her ladyship, after all, was destined to escape uninjured by my endeavors to effect her ruin. Was I right? You shall see.

"Nearly two years passed away, during which time, with the aid of my five hundred pounds, I had set up a first-rate public house in a populous and respectable neighborhood, and was making money. I have little doubt but that the sign of '*The Red Cask*' is still remembered in that vicinity—for that was the name which, actuated by a strange whim, I had given to my tavern; and the same was illustrated by a huge swinging sign in front, on which was painted the representation of a large cask overflowing with blood—which, I need scarcely tell you, was a sly and humorous allusion to the affair of Lagrange's murder.—Well, one cold, stormy winter's night, when the wind was howling like ten thousand devils around the house, I was seated in my comfortable tap-room, making myself extremely happy over a reeking jarum of hot rum punch. I was alone, for the hour was late, and all my guests had departed; when suddenly, during a pause in the clatter of the elements, I heard a low, timid knock at my outer door, which faced on the street.—Supposing it to be either some thirsty policeman, or a belated traveller anxious to escape from the fury of the storm, I arose and unbarred the door; as I opened it, a fierce gust of wind rushed in, so piercing cold, that it seemed to chill me to the very marrow of my bones; and at the same moment I beheld a human form crouching down under the narrow archway over the door, as if vainly endeavoring to shield herself from the fury of the tempest. I knew it was a woman, for I caught a glimpse at an old bonnet and tattered shawl. She shivered with the cold, which even made my teeth chatter, stout and rugged as I was. 'What do you want?' I demanded roughly—for I was impatient at having been thus unseasonably interrupted while paying my devotions to the mug of hot rum punch, in front of a rousing fire. As she made no immediate reply, I was about to bid her begone and shut the door, when she said, in a faint, yet earnest tone—'Oh, sir, for God's sake, as you hope for mercy yourself hereafter, let me come in for a moment—only a moment—that I may warm my benumbed and freezing limbs!' I paused a moment; I am not naturally hard-hearted, unless there is something to be gained by it; and besides, I felt a kind of curiosity to see what sort of a creature it was who wandered the streets that awful night, destitute and houseless; so I bade her come in, and with difficulty she followed me into the tap-room; placing a seat for her near the fire, I resumed my own, and while leisurely sipping my punch, a good opportunity was afforded me to examine her narrowly. She was probably about twenty years of age, but much suffering had made her look older. Though her features were worn and wasted, and though her cheeks were hollow by the pinchings of want, she was beautiful; her eyes were large, lustrous and eminently expressive, and two or three stray curls of luxuriant hair peeped from beneath her old, weather stained bonnet. Her form was tall, and graceful in its outlines; but what particularly struck me was the singular whiteness and delicacy of her hands, which plainly indicated that she had never been accustomed to labor of any kind. Her dress was wretched in the extreme, and was scarce sufficient to cover her nakedness, much less shield her from the inclemency of the weather,—nay, my inquisitive researches soon convinced me that the miserable gown she wore was, excepting an old shawl, her *only garment*—no under clothing, not even stockings,—and her feet (I noticed that they were small and symmetrical,) were only separated from the cold sidewalk by thin and worn-out shoes.—Yet, notwithstanding all her poverty and wretchedness, there was about her a look of subdued pride, which, though in strange contrast with her garb, well became her general air, and regular handsome features. Everything about her, excepting her dress, convinced me that she had fallen from better days, and, somehow, that look of pride struck me as being strangely familiar; yet I racked my brain in vain to recall from the dreamy past some image that I could identify with the female before me, who sat in front of my blazing fire and warmed her chilled limbs with every appearance of the most intense satisfaction.

"Her superior air commanded my involuntary respect. 'Madam,' said I, 'are you hungry?' She eagerly answered in the affirmative; I placed provisions before her, and she ate with an appetite almost ravenous. I then gave her some mulled wine, which seemed to revive her greatly; and she returned me her thanks in a manner so lady-like and refined (a manner, however, which insensibly partook of a peculiar and indirect kind of *hauteur*, as remarkable in her tone as in the expression of her features,) that I was more than ever satisfied that she had descended to her present wretched situation, certainly from a respectable, if not from a very superior, order of society.

"'You have benefitted me greatly, sir, and I thank you,' said she, inclining her head towards me with an air almost condescending. 'I assure you, you have not bestowed your *assistance* (she didn't say *charity*, observe!) upon a habitual mendicant or common person. I am by birth a lady; you will pardon me for declining to state the causes of my present condition. Again I thank you.'

"The devil, comrades! here was a starving, freezing beggar woman whom I had picked out of the street, and warmed and fed, playing the condescending, reserved lady, forsooth! and abashing and humbling me by her d——d lofty, proud looks! Ha, ha, ha! and yet I liked it, mightily; the joke was too good; and so I continued to 'madam' her, until at last I actually detected her on the very point of calling me 'fellow;' but fortunately for her, she checked herself in time to escape being turned into the street forthwith.

"And yet the superiority of her air and the haughtiness of her manner had for me an indescribable charm, no less than her beauty; and I resolved, if possible, to make her my mistress, for I doubted not that when she should become nourished and strengthened by proper food and rest, she would make a very desirable companion for a man of my amorous temperament. However, I did not broach the subject at that time, but contented myself with seeing that she was comfortably provided for that night, under the charge of one of the females of the house, to whom I gave money with which to provide the strange lady with proper and respectable clothing in the morning. The next day I had occasion to go away at an early hour, and did not return until late in the afternoon, and on entering my little parlor, I was surprised at beholding a lady, handsomely dressed, who advanced towards me with an air of dignified politeness. Her rich hair was most tastefully arranged; her neat dress closely fitted a slender but elegant shape, and I was struck with the dazzling fairness and purity of her complexion, and the patrician cast of her features. A second glance told me it was the female whom I had relieved the previous night; and I became aware of the fact that the strange lady was no other than Lady Adelaide Hawley!

"She did not recognize me, for I was much changed, in consequence of having removed the huge beard which I had worn, while in her husband's service. You may imagine my triumph at finding the proud lady an inmate of my house and a dependent on my bounty, under circumstances so humiliating to her and so gratifying to me; and you may well believe that I lost no time in giving her to understand the nature of the reward I expected in return for my hospitality. Would you believe it? She actually repulsed me with scorn, and began to talk of her birth, and the superiority of her rank to mine! Her confounded pride had now become altogether ridiculous; and somewhat enraged, I told her who I was. She started, regarded me for a moment with a scrutinizing look, and burst into tears, saying—'It is so, indeed! My punishment is just; I am humbled and degraded before the very menial I despised. Take, me, Simpson; do with me as you will; crime levels all ranks. Yet stay; I am still feeble; delay the consummation of your triumph for one week. During that period I shall regain the strength I have lost, and the beauty that has faded; then shall I be a fitting partner for your bed.' I consented; two or three days passed, and I was rejoiced to perceive that she daily grew in strength and beauty, and was fast regaining that voluptuousness of person which had formerly distinguished her. She related to me, at my request, the particulars of her downfall. She had been cast off by her husband and rejected by her relations with scorn and curses, when the fact of her adultery with St. Clair was discovered.—Entirely friendless and without resources, she was compelled to place herself under the protection of a gentleman of fashion and pleasure, who rioted on her luxuriant charms for a brief season, until possession and excess produced satiety, the sure forerunner of disgust—she was then thrown aside as a worthless toy, to make room for some fresh favorite. Rendered desperate by her situation, she became an *aristocratic courtezan*, freely sacrificing her person to every nobleman and gentleman of rank who chose to pay liberally for her favors. In this manner she subsisted for a time in luxury—but at last, her patrons (as is always the case) grew tired of her; she had become

> "Like a thrice-told tale,
> Vexing the dull ears of a drowsy man,"

and was again thrown upon the world without resources. Her indomitable pride still clung to her, through all her misfortunes; and though she plainly saw that her amours with the aristocracy were at an end forever, she disdained to seek meaner lovers among the humbler classes. Every offer made to her by men of medium rank, was spurned by the proud harlot with supreme contempt. 'I am a companion for nobility—not for the grovelling masses,' she would reply, in answer to all such offers; nor did the pinchings of want and hunger even for a moment shake her resolution, or disarm her prejudices. She might, had she been disposed, have still lived in comfort and even splendor, by becoming an inmate of some fashionable brothel; but as in such an establishment she would be required to bestow her favors indiscriminately on men of all ranks, who could pay for the same, she recoiled from the idea with disgust. Thus did the pride of this singular woman triumph over her wants and poverty; when on the very verge of starvation, with the means of relief within her grasp, the thought—'I am of noble birth,' would sustain her, and enable her to resist successfully the longings of hunger and the sufferings incidental to a homeless life. No scrupulous delicacy prevented her from accepting any assistance, pecuniary or otherwise, that might be offered to her; she even did not hesitate to ask for charity, in tones of *affected* humility; but the all-pervading principle, PRIDE OF BIRTH, implanted within her breast, imperiously restrained her from bestowing the favors of her patrician person upon 'vulgar plebeians;' and, in consequence, she had sunk lower and lower in want, destitution and misery, until driven, on that terrible winter's night, to supplicate for a slight and temporary relief at the door of one whom she had formerly so much despised, but on whom she was now so dependent.

"It was a cold evening, and her ladyship and myself were seated before a comfortable fire. An abundance of wholesome food, and every comfort which it was in my power to procure for her, had improved her appearance greatly. Her form had regained much of its natural roundness, and her countenance had recovered all its original beauty. She was gazing pensively into the fire; while I regarded *her* with an eye of admiration, and a heart full of amorous longings. At length I broke the silence. 'To-morrow night, madam,' said I, 'the week for which you stipulated, will have expired.' She sighed deeply, and murmured, in an almost inaudible tone, 'It is so, indeed.' Noticing the sigh which accompanied her words, a frown of displeasure gathered on my brow; but it was almost instantly dispelled, in the delight I felt at my approaching happiness. 'Yes,' I continued, 'to-morrow night I shall be the happiest of men; but madam, why delay until to-morrow night that felicity which may as well be enjoyed to-night? You can never be more beautiful or more voluptuous than you are at this moment.' During the utterance of these words, I had drawn my chair close to hers, and encircled her enchanting waist with my arm; I felt her heart throbbing wildly beneath my hand, which had invaded the snowy regions of her swelling charms—and I took it to be the wild throbbing of passion. We were alone—not a soul was stirring in the house; propitious moment! How longingly I gazed upon her dewy lips, which reminded me of the lines in Moore's *Anacreon*—which, I suppose, is all Latin and Greek to you, comrades:—

> "Her lips, so rich in blisses,
> Sweet petitioners for kisses!
> Pouting nest of bland persuasion,
> Ripely suing Love's invasion."

And they did not long sue in vain; for such vigorous salute as I gave them would have put even Captain St. Clair to the blush. While thus tasting the honey of the sweetest and most luscious pair of lips in the three kingdoms, I fancied that I felt her trembling with delight in my arms; but too soon did I become aware that she was only shuddering with disgust; for by a vigorous effort she struggled from my embrace, and, breathless and panting, said—'Not now, Simpson, not now, I entreat, I implore you! To-morrow night, the week's exemption which I craved, will be completed,—then—then—at this hour—you may—you will find me in my chamber; *then,* so help me God! I will offer no resistance; but now, not now!' I surveyed her ladyship with some surprise; her eyes sparkled like diamonds, and her face, neck and bosom were suffused with a ruddy, glowing hue. 'As you please, madam,' I coldly rejoined, for I was provoked at her violent and unexpected resistance—'as you please; but remember, I am no longer to be trifled with. To-morrow night be it, then; and see that you do not repeat this obstinacy of conduct, for I will then accomplish my object, even if I have to resort to force and violence!' *'I will not then resist you,* I swear it!' said she, with much solemnity of manner, and then added—'one favor I will ask of you: permit me to remain all day to-morrow in my chamber, and do not even attempt to see me, until twelve o'clock to-morrow night, at which hour you will find me waiting for your appearance.' I agreed to this request; and she bade me good-night in a tone almost cheerful, as she left the room to seek her chamber.

"The next day and the next evening passed;—the midnight hour arrived. I closed my house, and repaired to the chamber which had been assigned to the use of my lady guest. Finding the door unlocked, I softly entered the apartment; it was a spacious room, tolerably well furnished, and the bed was shrouded by muslin curtains; a lighted candle stood upon the table; glancing around I saw nobody. 'She is in bed,' thought I, and every nerve in my body thrilled with delight at the thought. I approached the bed, and drew aside the curtain. There she lay—but how very still! 'She sleeps,' thought I, somewhat surprised; and bending over in the dim light of the unsnuffed candle, I kissed her lips—heavens! what made them so very cold—and why was the hand which I had lasciviously laid upon her bosom, dampened with a warm liquid? I rushed to the table, seized the candle, and returned to the bed-side. There she lay—DEAD! The life-blood was welling from an awful gash in her left breast; her right hand grasped a dagger—the instrument of her death; the bed on which she lay was literally soaked with her blood, and my hand was stained with it. Then I comprehended her words—'*I will not then resist you!*' I staggered back, horror-stricken; the shadow of remorse for the first time darkened my soul; I would have wrested the dagger from her lifeless hand, and plunged it into my own heart, but in the agonies of death she had clutched it too firmly to admit of my easily tearing it from her grasp. I turned from the bed, and again placed the candle upon the table; I sat down by it, with the cold perspiration starting from every pore. Ha! what is this? a letter, and addressed to me? I had not observed it before. Eagerly I tore it open, and instantly recognized the elegant handwriting of her ladyship—not a blot, not a misformed letter marred the beautiful chirography of the missive; it was written with the same grace and precision that had in former days characterized her ladyship's notes of invitation to her splendid parties. As near as I can remember, it read as follows:—

"'Death is preferable to the dishonor of your vile embraces. Were you a man of birth, gladly would I accept the protection of your arms; but Lady Adelaide Hawley can never become the mistress of a menial. I welcome death, as it will preserve me from staining the purity of my noble blood by cohabitation with such as *thou* art. May heaven pity and forgive me!'

"After I had read this characteristic note, I reflected deeply upon the tragic event—her suicide. Innocent as I was of her death, might I not be arrested as her murderer?[B] Circumstances were strong against me; how could I prove my innocence? Many men have been hung on circumstantial evidence less strong. Though I had escaped detection on a murder which I had actually committed, I now feared that I should suffer for a deed of which I was not guilty. The gallows arose before my excited fancy, in all its terrors; my throat seemed encircled by the fatal rope.—I determined to fly the country; instantly acting upon this impulse, I left the chamber, and hastily collected together all my money (which was considerable) and valuables. Then I left the house, and seeking a safe asylum in an obscure party of the city, remained there until an opportunity was afforded me to take ship to America. I arrived here—soon spent all my money—was hauled up for a murder—was convicted of manslaughter only, and did the State service for a period of ten years in the stone institution at Charlestown; served out my time—and here I am. Now, comrades, you have heard my story; that it has been a long one, and a dry one, I grant—at all events, the narration of it has made *me* confoundedly dry. Here's a health to jolly thieves all the world over, and confusion to honesty, the law, and the police!"

[B] Acute and sagacious as Jew Mike was, it did not occur to him, in his trepidation and alarm, that the note which he had just read, and which was in Lady Hawley's own handwriting, would clearly exonerate him from all suspicion of his having murdered her. But guilt is sometimes singularly short-sighted, and Mike, as cunning a villain as he was, threw aside or perhaps destroyed the only evidence he could have possibly produced to substantiate his innocence.

Jew Mike did honor to his own toast in a bumper of brandy; nor were the others backward in following his example. Sow Nance, who had just awoke from a sound sleep, swore it was the most capital story she had ever heard in her life, which opinion she enforced by many oaths that we need not repeat. 'Charcoal Bill' and 'Indian Marth' were loud in their expressions of delight; and Jew Mike had the satisfaction of perceiving that he had pleased his audience, and made himself the hero of the night. A general conversation followed, which lasted until the Jew, as chairman of the meeting and Captain of the *Grabbers*, called the assembly to order, and announced that Sow Nance had the floor;—whereupon silence was restored, and that lady gave utterance to the following words, in a hoarse voice.—Her remarks were copiously interspersed with oaths, which, out of respect for the reader's feelings and our own credit, we omit:—

"Well, gals and fellers, being as how my Mike here has been a blowin' off his gas, I might as well blow mine. You all know how I first came to be se-duced, don't yer? It was a rich State street lawyer wot first did it, when I was 'leven years old. Ha, ha, ha! a jolly old cock he was, with a bald head and a face all over red pimples—he used to be mighty fond of us girls, I tell yer. Maybe I didn't use to suck the money out of him, by threatenin' to *blow* on him—well, I did! Yer all know how I had a young-'un, and how—ha, ha, ha!—the brat was found, the next day after it was born, dead in the *Black Sea*; it never died no nat'ral death that young-'un didn't, yer can bet yer life; the old Cor'ner wasn't far out of the way when he said in his werdict that the child had been strangled! The State street lawyer was its father, I believe, tho' I can't say for certain, I had so many partick'lar friends; for if I *ain't* werry good-looking, I've got winnin' ways. I came from a first-rate family, I did; my father was hung for killing my mother—one of my brothers has also danced a horn pipe in the air, and another is under sentence of death, off South, for beating a woman's brains out with a fire shovel, and choking her five children with a dishcloth. He's one of the true breed, he is. I ain't no dishonor to my family, either; for besides that strangling business, (mind, I didn't say *I* did it!) I once pitched a drunken sailor down stairs, which accidentally broke his neck, after I had lightened his pockets of what small change he had about him.—To tell the honest truth, I'm rather too ugly to make much money by doing business myself; so I've gone into the business of picking up young, good-looking gals, coaxing them off, and getting them into the houses of my regular customers, who pay me well, at so much a head. My best customer is the rich Mr. Tickels, who lives in South street; many's the young gal I've carried to him, and many's the dollar I've earned by it. Look here—do you see this five dollar gold piece? I earned it this morning by coaxing a gal to go with me to Mr. Tickel's house; she was a little beauty, I tell yer, and I'll bet she won't come out of that house the same as she went in, no how. She was a fruit gal, but she wasn't one of us; her name, I believe was Fanny—"

"Blood and battering-rams!"

This singular exclamation was made by the comical looking old man, who had entered the "Pig Pen" unperceived, and had been seated in the corner unnoticed by any of the company. He had arisen from his seat, and stood in an attitude which betokened profound interest and great astonishment. For a moment the whole gang, male and female, regarded him with surprise and suspicion; then Jew Mike sprang forward, seized him by the throat, shook him strongly, and in a rough, fierce voice, demanded:—

"Death and the devil, old scoundrel, how came you here? Who are you?—are you a police spy—one of Marshal Threekey's gang? Speak, d——n you, before I break every bone in your accursed old carcass!"

It was a singular contrast, between the great, powerful ruffian, and the little old man—nevertheless, the latter individual (who, the reader need scarcely be told, was no other than our eccentric friend, the Corporal,) did not tamely submit to such rough treatment; extricating himself, with much agility, from the grasp of the Jew, he dealt that worthy such a quick and stinging blow in the region of his left ear, that it laid him sprawling on the floor, at the same moment exclaiming—

"Skulls and skeletons! do you take me for a child? Nay, come on again, if you are so disposed, and by the nose of Napoleon! I'll beat you to a jelly!"

It is difficult to say what might have been the fate of the gallant Corporal, had a second encounter taken place, for the Jew arose from the floor with a howl of rage, his dark face livid with passion. But, fortunately for our friend, at this crisis there stepped forward a big, brawny, double-jointed Irishman, with a fist like a shoulder of mutton; this gentleman gloried in the title of 'Cod-mouth Pat,' in humorous allusion to the peculiar formation of his 'potato trap,' an aperture in his head which might have been likened either to a cellar door or a coal scuttle.

"Och, be the powers, Misther Jew Mike," said Pat, placing himself between the Corporal and his gigantic antagonist—"be asy, and lave the owld gintlman alone; he's a brave little man intirely, and it's myself that'll fight for him. Whoop! show me the man that 'od harm my friend, and be the holy poker, and that's a good oath, I'll raise a lump on his head as big as the hill of Howth, and that's no small one!"

The good-hearted Irishman's interference saved the Corporal from a severe beating, if not from being killed outright—for the Jew dared not engage in a personal conflict with a man of Pat's resolution and strength. Yet any ordinary observer could not have failed to notice the look of deadly vengeance that gleamed in his eyes, indicating that he would not soon forget or forgive the blow he had received.

At that moment, a loud noise resembling the crash of decanters and glasses, mingled with loud oaths and yells of defiance, which sounds proceeded from the adjoining dance cellar, plainly indicated that one of those "bloody rows" for which Ann street is famous, had commenced. Such a scene was too much the element of Cod-mouth Pat for him to remain tranquil during its progress; with an unearthly yell he grasped a short, thick cudgel which he always carried, and leaving the "Pig Pen," plunged into the thickest of the fight. Many a black eye and broken head attested the vigor of his arm; but the glory of his achievements did not screen him from being borne to the watchhouse, nor did his valor prevent the magistrate in the morning from inflicting upon him a very decent fine, which drew from him the indignant remark that—"'Tis a great country, any how, where a man can't have a ginteel bit of a fight without paying for it!"

The Corporal's case again looked desperate, when Pat left the "Pig Pen," for he was then without a protector from the vengeance of Jew Mike. But the Jew did not appear inclined to assail the old man personally, though his ferocious eyes still gleamed with rage. Standing apart, he held a whispered conversation with Sow Nance, during which the Corporal could occasionally overhear the words—'spy,' 'danger,' 'police,' 'murder,' and the like. At last they seemed to arrive at some definite conclusion; for the Jew came forward, and said—

"Old fellow, whoever you are, you have heard too much of our private discourse, for our safety.—We must confine you, until such time as you may succeed in convincing us that you meant no foul play in thus intruding into our secret rendezvous."

The Corporal began to speak, but the Jew fiercely commanded him to be silent. Meanwhile, Sow Nance had procured a rope, and ere the old man was aware of her intention, she had seized and pinioned his arms with great dexterity.

"Into the *Black Hole* with him!" shouted the Jew. The poor Corporal was hurried from the room, through a low, narrow door, along a dark, winding passage, and soon found himself in a spacious cellar, crowded with negroes, who were drinking "blue ruin" and smoking vile cigars. This resort of the "colored society" was a place of the most degraded and vicious kind, frequented by the lowest of the black population of Ann street. At that period, respectable public houses for the exclusive accommodation of the colored aristocracy, were very rare; and it is only recently that the enterprise and public spirit of Mr. William E. Ambush has established a *recherche* and elegant Saloon in Belknap street, bearing the poetical cognomen of "*The Gazelle.*" We allude to this latter place for the purpose of showing that however degraded may be the colored denizens of Ann street, and however low their resorts, there are nevertheless those of the same complexion who are elevated in their notions of propriety, and strictly exclusive in their associations.

"Hallo, here—where's Pete York?" demanded the Jew, looking around upon the sable assembly with an air of authority.

A small, very black and hideous looking negro stepped forward in answer to the name, with a grin that would not have disgraced the very devil himself.

"Dat's me, master," said he. (It may be as well to remark here, that this negro was soon afterwards sentenced to be hung for an atrocious murder, in Ann street. His sentence was, however, commuted by the Governor to imprisonment for life. He is now comfortably located in the Charlestown State Prison.)

"Well, then, you black scorpion, I wish you to take charge of this old fellow, and let him not escape, as you value your life. Keep him here safely for a day or two, and I'll reward you well for your trouble. Sooner than let him escape, *kill him*—do you hear?"

The negro *did* hear, and perfectly comprehended, also. He replied not in words, but in expressive pantomime. Drawing a knife from his belt, he passed his finger approvingly along its glittering edge—then he drew it lightly across his own throat, in the immediate vicinity of his windpipe; by which actions he meant to intimate that should the old gentleman, with whose guardianship he had the honor to be entrusted, manifest the least inclination to "give him the slip," he, Mr. Peter York, would, in the most scientific manner, merely cut his throat from ear to ear, as a particular token of his warm personal regard. Jew Mike appeared perfectly satisfied with the assurance thus eloquently conveyed, and, accompanied by Sow Nance, left the cellar, leaving the Corporal to the tender mercies of as desperate a band of villains and cut-throats as ever prowled about in the dark alleys and underground dens of Ann street.

"Now, my good fellow," said the old gentleman, addressing the negro whose prisoner he now was—"you had better instantly unbind me, and suffer me to take my departure from this infernal trap. Give me my liberty, and I will pay you ten times the sum that your Jew friend can afford to give you for detaining me here. What say you?"

"Oh, you shut up!" responded Pete York—"you s'pose I'm going to b'lieve any such gas as dat? You look like paying more money than Jew Mike, and not a decent coat on your back! Hush up your mouf, or you'll get this knife a-twixt your ribs in less than no time."

The black ruffian, in order to convince his prisoner that he meant what he said, pressed the sharp point of his knife so closely to the Corporal's breast, that it penetrated the skin. Mr. York, having thus practically admonished his victim to preserve silence, (which the Corporal thought it best to do, under the circumstances,) called to another negro, who was indulging in deep potations at the bar, in company with his "ladye love," a wench whose personal attractions consisted of a knotty head, flat nose, and mouth of immoderate dimensions—and that she *was* attractive to her lover, was afterwards manifested by the fact that in a fit of jealousy he murdered a rival in her affections; for which amusement he was hung in the yard of the Leverett street jail on the 25th day of May, 1849, in the presence of a very jovial party, who were highly delighted with the exhibition.

"Wash Goode," cried Mr. Peter York, addressing that gentleman with a familiar abbreviation of his patriotic Christian name—"look yeah, a moment, will you nigger?"

Mr. Washington Goode crossed the cellar, and desired to know in what way he could be serviceable to his particular friend and boon companion, Mr. Peter York. The latter gentleman explained himself in a few words.

"Jew Mike has put this old white man under my charge," said he, "for a few days, and I don't know where the h— —l to keep him. What shall I do with the old son of a— —?"

"Why, put him in de coal-hole, to be sure," replied the other, with a boisterous laugh at his own ingenious suggestion.

Mr. York signified his approval of this plan, and dragging the poor Corporal into the dark passage which he had traversed in going to the cellar, he seized a large iron ring, opened a trap door, and violently pushed his victim into the dark and yawning chasm. Then he shut down the trap door, securely fastened it and departed.

The unfortunate Corporal fell a distance of about eight feet, and landed upon a soft, damp bed of earth, with but little personal injury. It will be recollected that his arms had been pinioned by Sow Nance; but, by a desperate effort, the old man succeeded in freeing himself from his bonds. He then essayed to examine and explore the dismal pit into which he had been thrown—which, in the intense darkness that prevailed, was a task of no little danger. However, he cautiously began to grope about, and soon became satisfied that the place was of considerable extent.

It will readily be inferred that our friend Corporal Grimsby was a man of dauntless courage; but, notwithstanding this, a thrill of terror nearly paralysed his limbs, when, while exploring the dungeon into which he had been thrown, his feet came in contact with an object, which, on examination, he discovered to be a human skeleton. The dread of being left to starve and perish in that dismal den, in such awful company, well nigh overcame both his philosophy and courage; and seating himself upon the damp earth, he abandoned himself to those feelings of despondency naturally engendered by his situation.

A man placed in such circumstances, in the midst of intense darkness, can "take no note of time." An hour of horror will sometimes seem an age, while a week of unalloyed pleasure will often glide by seemingly with the same rapidity as a few fleeting moments. It may have been one hour—it may have been ten—that the Corporal sat on the floor of his dungeon; when suddenly he was startled by the noise of the trap-door above his head being opened, and looking up, he beheld Sow Nance gazing down upon him, holding in her hand a lantern. After regarding him intently for a few moments, she thus addressed him:—

"Say, old chap, what'll yer give me if I help yer to 'scape from this hole? Yer don't look as if yer had any money—but if yer have, pay me well, and I'll get you out."

"Lower down a ladder or a rope, and raise me from this infernal trap, and you shall have this purse—see, 'tis full of gold!" replied the Corporal, at the same time producing from his pocket a purse which was evidently well lined with the "needful."

Nance uttered an exclamation of surprise and pleasure, and then disappeared; in a few minutes she returned and lowered a ladder into the pit; the Corporal rapidly ascended, and soon stood at the side of his deliverer, whom he could not avoid thanking warmly, as he gave her the purse. Bidding him follow her, she conducted him through the dark passage; they entered the "Pig Pen," which was empty—passed through the dance cellar without attracting any attention, and to the intense joy of the Corporal, he found himself standing in the open air, with the sun shining brightly, and no one to hinder his departure from those corrupt regions of sin and horror.

He distinctly remembered that Sow Nance had boasted of having enticed a young girl to the abode of Mr. Tickels in South street. Now this latter individual was known to him as a libertine and a villain; and inwardly praying that he might not be too late to rescue his fair young friend (for he doubted not it was Fanny Aubrey,) from the power of such a monster, in season to preserve her virtue undefiled, he made the best of his way to South street. The reader knows how he rushed into the room just as Tickels was preparing to consummate the outrage, and how he laid the villain sprawling upon the floor, exclaiming—

"Broad-swords and bomb-shells! I am just in time!"

We have now seen the manner in which Corporal Grimsby discovered the whereabouts of Fanny Aubrey: and the mystery of his having arrived at a moment so very opportune, is explained.

Chapter V
The Chevalier and the Duchess

A period of six months elapsed, and it was now the month of June—voluptuous June, clad in the gorgeous livery of summer. A great change had taken place in the circumstances of several of the most prominent characters of our narrative. The grandfather of Fanny—the blind old basket-maker—had been "gathered to his fathers," and was sleeping in a humble but honorable grave. The excellent old Corporal, having seen the remains of his aged friend consigned to its kindred dust, had procured a comfortable and delightful asylum for the two orphans in the family of a valued friend of his—an elderly gentleman whom we shall call Mr. Goldworthy; he was a retired merchant, possessing an ample fortune, and was a widower, having an only daughter, with whom he resided in a splendid mansion in Howard street. Miss Alice Goldworthy, (then in her eighteenth year,) was one of those rare creatures who seldom bless this grovelling earth with their bright presence. She was truly an admirable combination of excellent personal and mental qualities, and possessed in an eminent degree that beautiful art (so seldom attained) of making all who came within the sphere of her genial influence, *perfectly happy*. But her most amiable characteristic was her good heart, which prompted her to entirely overlook every consideration of self, in her desire to benefit others. We have now, in our mind's eye, the exquisite original from whom we imperfectly draw this beautiful character; her pure soul looks gently forth from the azure depths of her soft eyes; lovely in her smile, for it is the glad sunshine of a happy heart—but has that heart ne'er known affliction or grief? Ah, yes; the harsh world hath, in former times, bruised that gentle sanctuary of all womanly virtue, by its rude contact; but an o'er-ruling Providence would not suffer the blighting storms of life to crush the sweet flower that bent resignedly to the blast—for the angels in heaven are not more pure and holy than she. Peace be with her, now and forever! and should her eyes e'er encounter these humble lines, she will pardon their unknown author for having ventured to gild his pages with her beautiful character—for he has gazed upon her as upon a star, shipping with a serene and softened lustre from the blue vault of heaven.

Her domestic accomplishments were not inferior to her social virtues. In the charming (because truthful) words of an unpretending but excellent poet—

> "She had read
> Her father's well-filled library with profit,
> And could talk charmingly; then she could sing
> And play, too, passably, and dance with spirit;
> Yet she was knowing in all needle-work,
> And shone in dairy and kitchen, too
> As in the parlor."

When Fanny Aubrey was ushered into the presence of this amiable young lady, she started with surprise and pleasure—for she instantly recognized in her the kind young lady who had presented her with the gold coin on the memorable day when she was entrapped by Sow Nance into the house of Mr. Tickels. The recognition was mutual; Miss Alice instantly remembered the pretty fruit girl whose appearance had so much interested her; and warmly did she welcome both the young orphans, as future inmates of her family. Fanny had never before lived in such a grand house, surrounded by every appliance of luxurious wealth; yet the unbounded kindness of Miss Alice and her worthy father soon placed her perfectly at her ease. Excellent teachers were provided for her and her brother Charles—and, under the fostering care of their generous patrons, they promised to become ornaments to the elevated sphere of society in which they were probably destined to move.

Time passed on, and nothing occurred to interrupt the smooth current of Fanny's existence, until it was deemed advisable to engage a person properly qualified to give her instructions on that indispensable fixture to a fashionable parlor—the piano-forte. A teacher of some reputed talent was employed for this purpose; he was a Mr. Price, of Charlestown—and has since rendered himself somewhat famous for his amours in the above city with a married lady whom we shall call Mrs. Stout; he had for some time been giving her lessons on the piano—but the husband suspected that he was in the habit of imparting to her secrets more profound than those of music; he accordingly placed himself in a position to observe the operations of the parties—and soon detected them under circumstances of a very unequivocal character. Rushing in, he severely castigated the gay Lothario, who, laboring under the great disadvantage of having his costume seriously disarranged, could only implore for mercy, while he assumed the abject posture so faithfully depicted by a talented artist, in the engraving which accompanies this chapter. Long previous to this humorous event, Mr. Price was, as we have stated, engaged to instruct the pretty Fanny Aubrey in the science and mystery of the noble instrument of which he was a well-known professor; but he soon began to indulge in such alarming familiarities with his fair pupil, that she acquainted her friends with his conduct, and the consequence was that Mr. Price received a very dishonorable dismissal from the house. Nature has been very miserly of her favors to this amorous music teacher: his countenance resembles that of an unwashed charcoal merchant, while his manners are utterly devoid of anything like gentlemanly refinement.—We are no great critic of the art of piano teaching; but we opine that it is rather unnecessary, in the first stages of the instruction, to clasp a lady's waist, or even to bring one's mouth in too close proximity to her rosy lips. It leads a sensitive female, or a fastidious gentleman to suspect the existence of a strong desire to enjoy a more familiar intimacy with a feminine pupil, and is apt to result in the teacher's ignominious ejection from the house and family which he attempts to dishonor.

With the exception of Mr. Price's insults, (from which she easily escaped by appealing to her kind patrons for protection,) Fanny's life passed on happily and quietly for some time; until one evening, on entering the parlor, she was startled by seeing no less a person than the Hon. Timothy Tickels, of South street, in familiar and friendly conversation with Mr. Goldworthy and Miss Alice. Mr. Tickels himself started and turned pale on beholding the maid whom he had attempted to dishonor under circumstances of such peculiar atrocity; however, he quickly recovered himself, and bowed low as Mr. Goldworthy presented her to him, saying—

"Mr. Tickels, this is Miss Aubrey, the young lady whom I spoke to you about, as having recently come to reside with me. Fanny, this is an old and much esteemed friend of mine, who has expressed a great desire to see you, and whom, I am sure, you will love and respect for his piety and moral excellence!"

Fanny coldly returned the salutations of the lecherous old hypocrite, whom she had such a good reason to hate and despise; it was evident to her that he had imposed on her worthy patrons, who really believed him to be a man of unblemished moral and religious character. During the evening, other company came in, and Tickels, having placed himself at Fanny's side, whispered in her ear—

"My dear young lady, I see you recognize me; I also knew you instantly; for God's sake do not expose me! I am sincerely sorry for the wrong I meditated against you—I have since repented in sackcloth and ashes. Promise me, I entreat you, that you will not whisper a word in regard to that infamous affair to Miss Alice or her father—or, indeed, to any one else; promise me, angel that you are—will you not?"

Fanny reflected a few moments, during which she asked herself—"What is the right course for me to pursue in this matter? It will be very wrong for me to ruin this man by exposing him, if he has sincerely repented. The Bible tells us to forgive our enemies—ought I not to forgive him? Yes, I will; my heart and conscience tell me it will be right to do so. Mr. Tickels," she added, aloud—"I forgive you for having tried to injure me, and, if you have truly repented, I will never say anything about the affair which you wish to have kept secret."

How artlessly and ingenuously she pronounced those words of forgiveness, to a man who had tried to inflict upon her the greatest injury that can befall woman—a man who, even at that moment, in the black hypocrisy of his heart, gloated upon her youthful charms as the wolf doth feast his savage eyes upon the innocent lamb! Yes, and even at that moment, too, his polluted soul was hatching an infernal plan to get her again in his power, in a place where no aid was ever likely to wrest her from his grasp—a place established for purposes of lust and outrage, to which he had alluded, (in his soliloquy after the rescue of Fanny by the Corporal,) as the "Chambers of Love."

"Ah, my young paragon of virtue," said the old hypocrite to himself—"it is all very well for you to prate of forgiveness; but I'll have you in the 'Chambers' in less than a month—then see if you can again escape me! In that luxurious underground retreat, from whose mysterious recess no cry can reach the ears of prying mortals above—there, amid the sumptuousness of an Oriental palace, will I riot on those charms of thine, which now I dare but gaze upon! I'll make thee a slave to every extravagant caprice of my passion; I'll become a god of pleasure, and thou, my beautiful blonde, shall be my ministering angel; for me shalt thou fill the glittering wine-cup with the sparkling gem of the grape; for me shalt thou sing at the banquet, and preside as Venus at the rosy couch of love."

Such were the thoughts that passed through the mind of the disgusting old voluptuary, while his lying tongue gave utterance to words like the following:—

"A thousand thanks, my kind young lady, for that promise! Ah, if you only knew how beautiful you are, you would not so much blame me for my folly—my wickedness. But I'll say no more, as such language seems to pain you. I have, by long fasting and sincere prayer, succeeded in cleansing my heart from every impure desire—I can now view you with the holy feelings—the passionless regard, of a father for his daughter. My dear child, forget not your promise to refrain from exposing an erring fellow mortal; and may Heaven bless you!"

Poor, unsuspecting Fanny!—could she have seen the black heart of the smooth villain who addressed her with such pious humility, how well she might have exclaimed, with Byron—

> "Thy love is lust, thy friendship all cheat,
> Thy smiles hypocrisy, thy words deceit."

Mr. Tickels continued to visit the Goldworthys frequently; and they, far from suspecting his real character, always received him with the familiarity of an old friend. They noticed that Fanny treated him with marked coolness and reserve; this they thought but little of, however, merely regarding it as an excess of diffidence.

It is now necessary that we introduce a new character on the stage. This was a gentleman who bore the rather aristocratic title of the "Chevalier Duvall," and was supposed to be a foreigner of distinguished birth; and if noble lineage ever indicated itself by splendid personal or mental gifts, then was the Chevalier entitled to the fullest belief when he declared himself to have descended from one of the noblest families of France—for a man of more superb and commanding beauty never won the heart of a fair lady. We confess ourselves rather opposed to the prevailing tastes of authors, who make all their heroes and heroines perfect paragons of personal beauty—but, in the present instance, we are dealing, not with an imaginary creation, but with an actual character. The Chevalier, then, was a man of a thousand; elegant in his carriage, superbly graceful in every movement, possessing a form of perfect symmetry, and a countenance faultlessly handsome, no wonder that he captivated the hearts of many lovely damsels, and made no unfavorable impression upon the mind of the fair Alice Goldworthy, whom he had casually met in polished society, and whose admiration he had enlisted, as much by the charms of inimitable wit as by the graces of his matchless person. What wonder that the gentle girl, all unskilled as she was in the ways of the world, should receive his frequent visits with pleasure; and when her kind father intimated to her that her lover was a man possessing no visible resources, and was besides very unwilling to allude to his former history, which was involved in much obscurity, what wonder that she made herself his champion, and assured her father that he (the Chevalier) was everything that the most fastidious could desire. And the good old man, never very inquisitive or meddlesome in what he considered the affairs of others, and satisfied that his daughter's views of her lover must be correct, forbore to pain her further by any insinuations derogatory to the Chevalier's character, and made no objections to his oft-repeated visits.

Delicious was that dream of love to the pure-hearted maiden! Her lover was to her the *beau ideal* of manhood; so delicate in his attentions, so uniformly respectful in his behavior. What if mystery *did* exist in reference to his history and resources?—when did Love ever stop to make inquiries relative to descent or dollars? As long as she believed Duvall to be an honorable and good man, she would have deserted her luxurious home and shared poverty and exile with him, if necessary. Ah, how often does Love, in the best and purest natures, triumph over filial affection and every consideration of worldly or pecuniary advantage.

"My Alice," said Duvall, as they were seated in Mr. Goldworthy's luxurious parlor, at that most delightful period of the day—twilight—bewitching season, when day softly melts into the embrace of night!—"*My Alice, there is much connected with my name and fortunes that must be to you a profound mystery; but, believe me, my name is untainted with dishonor, and my fortunes are free from disgrace. A solemn vow prevents me from explaining myself further, until the blissful moment when I can call you wife; then, idol of my soul, shall you know all. Behold this right hand; it has never committed an action that could make this cheek blush with shame. And now, fairest among women, when shall I claim this soft hand as my own lawful prize?"

The day was named, and the happy Alice was for the first time clasped to the bosom of her lover.

At the hour of noon, on the next day, a gentleman might have been standing on the steps of the Tremont House, gazing with an eye of abstraction upon the passing throng. The age of this gentleman might have been a matter of dubious inquiry; he was not young, you'd swear at the first glance, and yet, after you had gazed two minutes into his superb countenance, you would be as ready to swear that he was not over thirty, or thirty-five at most. In truth, he was one of those singular persons whose external appearance defies you to form any opinion as to their age, with any hope of coming within twenty years of the truth. Not a single gray hair could be seen among the glossy curls that fell over his noble forehead—not a wrinkle disfigured the smooth surface of his dark, beautiful skin—and yet there was *something* that we cannot define or describe, in the expression of his eyes, which now flashed with all the fire of youth, and then grew almost dim as with the shadows of advancing age—a something that indicated to any acute observer that the elegant stranger had passed the prime of manhood.

He was dressed with tasteful simplicity. A splendid black suit set off his fine form to advantage; yet his attire was utterly devoid of ornament. Many were the bright eyes that glanced admiringly at his handsome person; yet he seemed unconscious of the admiration he excited, and gazed upon the passing crowd with all the calm complacency of a philosopher.

This gentleman was the Chevalier Duvall. Not long had he been standing upon the steps of the Tremont House, when he was accosted by an elderly gentleman of a portly appearance, whom he cordially greeted with every token of familiar friendship.

The portly old gentleman was the Honorable Timothy Tickels; he and the Chevalier had long been intimate friends, having frequently met at the house of Mr. Goldworthy. After the usual compliments, Mr. Tickels remarked to his friend—

"By the way, my dear Chevalier, you remember that you long since promised to introduce me to a sister of yours, whose charms you highly extolled. I am anxious to see if she really merits your somewhat extravagant praise. I have a few hours of leisure to-day, and if you will present me to her, I shall be delighted."

"Certainly, my good sir, certainly," rejoined the Chevalier—"the distance is but trifling, and if you will do me the honor to accompany me, to my humble abode, you shall be made acquainted with the most beautiful woman in Boston. My sister is called the *Duchess*, and as mystery is the peculiar characteristic of myself and family, you will have the kindness to address her by that title."

Mr. Tickels expressed his thanks; and the two gentlemen proceeded to Somerset street, wherein stood the residence of the Chevalier. It was a house of modest exterior, very plain but respectable in appearance; yet the interior was furnished very handsomely. On entering the house, Duvall directed a servant to inform the Duchess that he had brought a gentleman to be introduced to her; and in about a quarter of an hour the lady sent word that she was prepared to receive her brother and his friend in her *boudoir*. Accordingly, the gentlemen ascended to that apartment; and on entering, Mr. Tickels stood for a few moments rooted to the floor with astonishment.

It was a small chamber, but furnished with every indication of the most exquisite taste. Fresh flowers, smiling from beautiful vases, scented the air with their delicious perfume; classic statuary adorned every corner, and gorgeous drapery at the windows excluded the glare of day, producing a kind of soft twilight. Voluptuous paintings, with frames superbly carved and gilded, ornamented the walls; and the footsteps fell noiseless on the rich and yielding Turkish carpet. A splendid harp and piano evinced the musical taste of the tenant of that elegant retreat.

But it was not the fragrance of flowers, or the beauties of sculpture, or the divine skill of the painter, that enthralled the senses of Mr. Tickels, and caused him to pause as if spell-bound in the centre of the room. No—his gaze was riveted upon a female form that reclined upon a sofa; and now we are almost inclined to throw down our pen in despair, for we are conscious of our inability to describe such a glorious perfection of womanly beauty as met the enraptured gaze of a man, whose sensual nature amply qualified him to appreciate such charms as she possessed.

She was not what the world calls a *young* woman; yet thirty years—thirty summers—had not dim'd the lustre of her beauty. Truly, she was the VENUS OF BOSTON! A brow, expansive and intellectual—hair of silken texture, that fell in massive luxuriance from beneath a jewelled head-dress which resembled the coronet of a duchess—cheeks that glowed with the rosy hue of health and a thousand fiery passions—eyes that sparkled with that peculiar expression so often seen in women of an ardent, impetuous nature, now languishing, melting with tender desires, now darting forth arrows of hate and rage—these were the characteristics of the Duchess! There she lay, the very personification of voluptuousness—large in stature, full in form, and exquisitely beautiful in feature! Her limbs (once the model of a renowned sculptor at Athens,) would have crazed Canova, and made Powers break his "Greek Slave" into a thousand fragments; and those limbs—how visible they were beneath the light, transparent gauze which but partially covered them! Her leg, with its exquisite ankle and swelling calf,—faultless in symmetry,—was terminated by a tiny foot which coquettishly played with a satin slipper on the carpet,—a slipper that would have driven Cinderella to the commission of suicide. Her ample waist had never been compressed by the wearing of corsets, or any other barbarous tyranny of fashion; yet it was graceful, and did not in the least degree approach an unseemly obesity; and how magnificently did it expand into a glorious bust, whereon two "hillocks of snow" projected their rose-tinted peaks, in sportive rivalry—revealed, with bewildering distinctness, by the absence of any concealing drapery! When she smiled, her lips, like "wet coral," parted, and displayed teeth of dazzling whiteness, and when she laughed, she did so *musically*. Her hand would have put Lord Byron in extacies, and her taper fingers glittered with costly gems. Such was the glorious creature who entranced the senses of the Honorable Timothy Tickels on entering her luxurious *boudoir*.

She greeted her brother the Chevalier with a smile, and his friend with a graceful inclination of her head; but she did not arise, for which she apologized by stating that she was afflicted with a slight lameness caused by a recent fall. Then she glided into a discourse so witty, so fascinating, that Mr. Tickels was charmed beyond expression.

"I must really chide you, Chevalier," said she, turning to her brother—"for not having afforded me the gratification of an earlier introduction to your friend; for I now have the honor of making his acquaintance under extremely unfavorable circumstances;—almost an invalid, and arrayed in this slovenly *dishabille*. My dear Mr. Tickels," she added, "you must not look at me, for I am really ashamed of having been caught in this deplorable plight."

Admirable stroke of art!—to apologize to an accomplished libertine, for liberally displaying to his amorous gaze charms that would have moved a marble statue!

"Magnificent Duchess," quoth Mr. Tickels, drawing nearer to her, and eagerly surveying the exposed charms of her splendid person—"offer no apology for feasting my eyes on beauty such as yours. I am no fulsome flatterer when I declare to you, that you are the queen and star of all the beautiful women it has ever been my lot to behold! You are not offended at my familiarity?"

The Duchess only said "fie!" and pouted for a moment, so as to display her ripe lips to advantage; and then her face became radiant with a smile that made Mr. Tickels' susceptible heart beat against his ribs like the hammer on a blacksmith's anvil.

The Chevalier rose. "You must excuse me, both of you," said he, as he took up his hat—"I have got an engagement which will oblige me to deprive myself of the pleasure of your agreeable company for the present. So *au revoir*—make yourself perfectly at home, my dear Mr. Tickels; and it will be your own fault if you do not ripen the intimacy which has this day commenced between yourself and the Duchess."

The Chevalier departed, and Mr. Tickels was alone with the magnificent Duchess.

The old libertine spoke truly when he declared that he had never before seen such a beautiful woman. Accustomed as he was to the society of ladies, in whose company he always assumed a degree of familiarity that was almost offensive, he was nevertheless so awed and intoxicated by the divine loveliness of the Duchess, that, when he found himself alone with her, he completely lost his usual self-possession, and could only declare his admiration by his glances—not by words. For a few minutes she coquettishly toyed with her fan—then she carelessly passed her jewelled hand over her queenly brow to remove the clustering hair; and finally, with an arch glance, she complimented Mr. Tickels on his taciturnity, and laughingly enquired if he was always thus silent in the society of ladies?

"Madam," replied Mr. Tickels—"I am struck dumb by your unsurpassable beauty. Forgive me, but my tongue is mute in the presence of such a divinity."

"Fie, sir! I must scold you if you flatter me," responded the Duchess, as her cheeks were suffused with a charming blush—"and yet I find it very hard to be angry with you, for your compliments are clothed in language so elegant, that they are far from being odious. Here is my hand, in token of my forgiveness."

She gave him her hand—a hand so white, so soft, so exquisitely delicate, that its touch thrilled through the entire frame of Mr. Tickels. Involuntarily he raised it to his lips, and knelt down before her;—then suddenly recollecting himself, he arose, murmuring a confused apology for his rudeness. Her brilliant eyes were turned upon his, with a soft expression, like that of languishing desire; and partly rising from the sofa, she made room for Mr. Tickels to seat himself at her side. This action she accompanied by a gesture of invitation; and eagerly did the old gentleman sink down upon the soft and yielding sofa. At first he sat at a respectful distance from her; but gradually he edged closer and closer, until their persons touched. Still she manifested not the slightest displeasure; and at last, maddened by his close proximity to such matchless charms—for lust very often triumphs over prudence—he ventured to steal his arm around her voluptuous waist. To his inexpressible delight, she did not repulse him; and then how wildly palpitated his heart, as he gazed down into those swelling regions of snow, within whose mysterious depths a score of little Cupids might have nested! Bolder and bolder grew the excited old voluptuary, as he found that she did not resist his amorous advances; her fragrant breath fanned his cheek, and the glances of her lustrous eyes dazzled his senses. Her ripe lips were provokingly near to his—why not taste their nectar? He pressed her closer to him, and she turned her charming face full towards him, and seemed, with an arch smile, to challenge him to bear off the prize. One little inch alone intervened between her rosy mouth and his own *watering* one; in a moment 'twas done! He had stolen a kiss, and received in return a playful tap with her fan. Who, that has once ravished a kiss from the divine lips of a lovely woman, does not feel inclined to repeat the offence? Again and again he kissed her; and finally, almost beside himself with rapture, he glued his hot lips to her neck, her shoulders, her bosom. Then Mr. Tickels became sensible that he had gone too far—for she disengaged herself from his embrace, and said, with an air of offended dignity—

"You seem to forget yourself, sir; my foolish complacency to the friend of my brother has, I fear, led me to permit liberties, which have engendered in your breast desires injurious to my honor. I confess that I was, for a moment, overcome by certain feelings which I possess, in common with all others of the human family; nay, I will even admit that I am of a nature peculiarly ardent and susceptible; and your refined gallantry, and my close contact with your really very agreeable person, aroused my passions, and caused me to forget my prudence until your liberties became so intimate that I feared for the safety of my honor. I must not forget my position as a lady of character and birth; and I trust that you will remember your pretensions to the title of a gentleman."

"Forgive me, beautiful Duchess," cried Tickels, in tones the most abject—"on my bended knees I implore your pardon. What man, possessing heart and soul, could view such heavenly charms as thine, without being betrayed into an indiscretion? But forgive me, and I will ask no greater favor than to be allowed to kiss that beauteous hand."

"I am not angry with you," said the Duchess, giving him her hand, which he raised reverently to his lips, "for I can fully appreciate the feelings which prompted your conduct; therefore, I willingly forgive,—and now that we are good friends again, you may come and sit by my side, provided you will promise to be very good, and neither kiss me or clasp my waist with your arm. So, sir, that is very well—but why do you gaze so intently at my pretty shoulders and—but, good heavens! until this moment I was unconscious of my almost naked condition; if you will persist in looking at me, I must positively cover myself with a shawl."

"Charming Duchess, that would be worse sacrilege than to cover a costly jewel with tow-cloth," rejoined Tickels; and the lady smiled at his gallantry, as she remarked—

"Nevertheless, naughty man, you must not take advantage of my negligent and slight attire to devour my person with your eyes. Besides, I am too *em bon point* for either grace or beauty, and am naturally anxious to conceal that defect."

"Defect!" exclaimed Tickels,—"if there is one single defect in your glorious person, then is Venus herself a pattern of ugliness. The voluptuous fullness of your form is your most delightful attribute."

A silence of some minutes ensued, during which the old libertine continued his longing gaze, while the lady took up and fondly caressed a beautiful little lap-dog, whose snowy fleece was prettily set off by a silver collar, musical with bells. How Tickels envied the little animal, when its mistress placed it in her bosom, and bestowed upon it every epithet of tender endearment!

"Poor Fido!" at length said the lady, with a soft sigh,—"thou art the sole companion of my solitude. You would scarcely believe, Mr. Tickels, how devotedly I am attached to this little creature, and how much he loves me in return. He will only take his food from my hand, and I feed him on the most delicate custards. Every morning I wash him carefully in rose water, and he is my constant bed-fellow at night. ('Lucky dog!' sighed Tickels.) I have only his society to dispel the *ennui* of my solitude;—but, now I think of it, I have other sources of amusement: for there are my books, my music, my flowers. By the way, are you fond of music? Yes, I know you are; for you are a gentleman of too much elegant refinement of mind, not to love the divine harmony of sweet sounds. And now I shall put your gallantry to the test by requesting you to bring my harp hither; and to reward you for your trouble, you shall hear a song."

The instrument was placed before her, and she sang, with exquisite feeling and pathos, the beautiful song commencing with—

"'Twere vain to tell thee all I feel,
Or say for thee I sigh."

Tickels, to do him justice, was a true connoisseur in music; and warmly did he express his gratification at the performance, particularly as the Duchess accompanied the words by glances expressive of every tender emotion.

"Heigho! what can have become of the Chevalier? Devoted as he is to the erratic pursuits of a man of fashion, he is seldom at home, and consequently I see but little of him." Thus spoke the Duchess, after a long pause which had begun to be embarrassing.

"Do you long for his return?" asked Tickels—"will not my society compensate for his absence?"

"Oh, yes!" laughingly replied the lady—"you are gallant and agreeable; whereas my brother is often moody and abstracted. Besides, you know, a *brother* cannot of course be such a pleasant companion to a lady, as—as—I had almost said a *lover*. In truth, I am willing to confess that you are a dear, delightful old gentleman, and I am half in love with you already. Nay, don't squeeze my hand so, or I shall repent having made the declaration."

"You are a sweet creature," rejoined Tickels—"and very cruel for having afforded me a glimpse of heaven, and then shut out the prospect from my longing gaze. But tell me, how is it that you and your brother are so completely isolated in society? Certainly you must have relatives and many friends; yet you complain of solitude. If my question is not impertinent, will you tell me?—for a woman of your extraordinary beauty and accomplishments never finds it difficult to surround herself with a circle of admirers, and loneliness is an evil with which she never need be afflicted. To say merely that I feel interested in you, would fail to express the degree of admiration with which I regard you; and it would afford me an unspeakable pleasure to hear the history of your life, from those rosy lips."

"Alas!" exclaimed the Duchess, as a tear dim'd for a moment the lustre of her fine eyes—"my story is but a short and sad one. Such as it is, however, you shall have it. I was born beneath the fair skies of sunny France; my parents were noble and rich—my father, the Duke D'Alvear, could even boast of royal blood in his veins, while my mother was closely allied to several of the most aristocratic families in the kingdom. Reared in the lap of luxury, my childhood passed like a pleasant dream, with nothing to disturb its quiet, until I had reached my fifteenth year, at which period I lost both my parents by a catastrophe so sudden, so dreadful, that when you hear its particulars, you will not blame me for weeping as I do now." Here the lady's voice was broken by many sobs—but she soon recovered her composure, and continued her narrative.

"My mother was beautiful but frail—which was in her case peculiarly unfortunate, for my father was the most jealous of men. He had reason to suppose that a handsome young Count was too intimate with her; keeping his suspicions profoundly secret, he made preparations for a long journey, and having announced his intention of remaining abroad several months, he departed from Paris. That very night, at midnight, he abruptly returned, proceeded directly to my mother's chamber, and found the Count St. Cyr in her arms. The guilty pair were taken too much by surprise to attempt resistance or escape, and both were slain on the spot by my father, who had provided himself with weapons for that purpose. The Duke then went to his own chamber—the report of a pistol was heard soon afterwards, and the unfortunate man was found dead, with his brains scattered over the carpet.

Thus in one fatal night were my only brother and myself made orphans—nor was this our only misfortune, for the notary who had the charge of our joint patrimony, absconded, and left us penniless. Why need I dwell on the painful details of our poverty and its attendant miseries? Suffice it to say that I resisted a hundred offers from men of rank and wealth, who would have maintained me in luxury had I consented to part with the priceless gem of my virtue. Yes—I resisted each tempting proposal, for poverty itself was sweeter to me than dishonor. We came to America, and finally to Boston; the Chevalier, by giving private lessons in the sword exercise, supports us both in a style of quiet comfort—but I charge you, sir, never let that fact be known, for the gossiping world must never learn that the son of France's proudest noble has so degenerated as to *labor* for his support. Of course, with our modest means, we can mix but little in the gay and fashionable world—as for myself, I prefer to remain at home, and see but few persons except my brother and such of his intimate friends as he occasionally brings home with him. My retired habits have preserved me from the matrimonial speculations of gentlemen, of which I am very glad, for I do not think I shall ever marry; and the seclusion of my life has also saved me from the dishonorable proposals of amorous gentlemen, who are ever ready to insult a good-looking woman provided she is poor, and they are wealthy. Unfortunately for me, I have a constant craving for male society; and when thrown into the company of an agreeable man, be he young or old, passions which have never been gratified will assert their supremacy in my breast, and I often tremble lest, in a moment of delirium, I surrender my person unresisting to the arms of a too fascinating seducer. This weakness of my ardent nature has already several times nearly brought me to ruin; and when your arms just now encircled me, and your lips were pressed to mine, the dizzy delight which I experienced would, in a few moments, have made me your victim, had I not, by a powerful effort, overcome that intoxication of my senses which was fast subduing me; I escaped from your arms, and thank heaven! my honor is preserved. Now, sir, I have frankly told you all; you certainly will not censure me for my misfortunes—and I trust you will not blame me for those propensities of nature to which we are all subject, and which are so peculiarly strong in me as to render their subjection an act of heroic self-denial."

Thus ended the narrative of the Duchess; and it may well be imagined that her words inflamed the passions of her listener more than ever. To have that splendid creature sit by his side, and candidly confess to him that the ardor of her soul yearned for enjoyments which cold prudence would not permit her to indulge in,—what could have been more provoking to his already excited feelings? Mr. Tickels gazed earnestly at her for a few minutes, and his mind was decided; he resolved, if possible, to *reason* her into a compliance with his wishes.

"Madam," said he, assuming a tone of profound respect—"you are an educated and accomplished lady; your mind is of the most elevated and superior order. You can reflect, and reason, and view things precisely as they are, without any exaggeration. Look abroad upon the world, and you will see all mankind engaged exactly alike—each man and woman is pursuing that course which he or she deems best calculated to promote his or her happiness; and happiness is the essence of *pleasure*. Your miser hoards gold—that is *his* source of pleasure; your vain woman seeks pomp, and display, and adorns her person with many jewels—from all of which she derives *her* pleasure; and as the child is pleased with its rattle, so is the musty antiquarian with his antique models—so is the traveller with his journeyings and explorations—so is the soldier with glory—and so is the lady of warm impulses with her secret amours. All seek to extract pleasure from the pursuit of some darling object most congenial with their passions, their tastes, their preferences. Why, then, should any one seek to set aside the order of things universal—the routine of nature? As consistently might we disturb the harmonious operation of some complex machinery, as to act in opposition to the great fundamental law of human nature—viz: *that every created being, endowed with a ruling passion, should seek its legitimate gratification.* By legitimate gratification, I mean, that indulgence which interferes not with the enjoyments or interests of others. The miser should not accumulate his gold at the expense of another; the libertine should not revel in beauty's arms, by force; the lady must make a willing sacrifice—thus nobody is injured—and thus the pleasure is *legitimate*; though bigoted churchmen and canting hypocrites may declaim on the sin of carnal indulgences unsanctioned by the priest and his empty ceremonies. Fools! NATURE, and her laws, and her promptings, and her desires, spurn the trammels of form and custom, and reign triumphant over the hollow mummery of the parson and his pious foolery.

"Now, dear madam," continued the artful logician, (whose words belied his own sentiments, and his own belief,) "supposing that you admit all these premises; what do we next arrive at? Let me be plain, since you have been so candid with me. You have admitted that the prevailing and all-absorbing passion of your nature is—an intense desire to enjoy that delicious communion which had its origin in the garden of Eden. Why deprive yourself of the gratification you long for? Why do you hunger for the fruit which is within your reach? Why disregard the promptings of nature? Why obstinately turn aside from a bliss which is the rightful inheritance of every man and woman on the face of the earth? And, lastly, why are you so cruel to me, whom you have been pleased to pronounce agreeable? Answer me, charming Duchess, and answer me as your own generous heart and good sense shall dictate."

The Duchess was silent for a short time, and appeared to reflect profoundly; then she said, in a tone and manner singularly earnest—

"Listen to me, my friend—for that you are such, I am very sure. I do not deprive myself of the pleasures of which you speak, in consequence of any scruples, moral or religious. I have no respect for the institution of matrimony, or its obligations; I laugh at the doctrines of those who speak of the crime of an indulgence in Love's pleasures, without the sanction of the church. I agree with you that we all have derived from nature the *right* to feed our diversified passions according to their several cravings; but while we are authorized, by the very laws of our being, to seek those delights of sense for which we yearn, a perverted and ridiculous PUBLIC OPINION prohibits such indulgences, unless under certain restrictions, and accompanied by certain forms. Now, though this public opinion undoubtedly *is* ridiculous and perverted, it must nevertheless be respected, particularly by a lady; otherwise the world, (which is public opinion,) calls her a harlot—points at her the finger of scorn—excludes her from all decent society, and she is forever disgraced and ruined. I must preserve my reputation and position as a lady, no matter at what cost, or what sacrifice; ardently as I long for the delights of love, I shall never, to enjoy them, surrender my personal freedom by marriage, or my character by yielding to the solicitations of a lover,—unless, in the latter case, I should unfortunately, while in the intoxication of excited passion, grant the favors which he asks; which I pray heaven may never happen to me! It is all very well, sir," continued the Duchess, assuming a tone of arch vivacity—"it is all very well for you *men* to be in such continual readiness to indulge in the joys of Venus, whenever opportunity presents itself; for this odious public opinion is very lenient with you, gay deceivers that you are, and kindly pardons and even smiles at your amorous frailties; but we poor women, good heavens! must not swerve six inches from the straight path of rectitude marked out for us, under pain of eternal condemnation and disgrace; and thus we are either driven into matrimony, or are obliged to deprive ourselves of a bliss (to use your own language) which is the rightful inheritance of every man and woman on the face of the earth. Well," added the Duchess, in a tone of mock melancholy which was irresistibly charming,—"poor *I* must submit to the stern decree, as well as the rest of those unfortunate mortals called women;—unfortunate because they *are* women, and because they are even more ardent in their passions than those who have the happiness to be men. Let me congratulate you, sir, on your felicity in belonging to a sex which possesses the exclusive privilege of unrestricted amative enjoyment; and I am sure you will not refuse to sympathize with me on my misfortune, in having been born one of those wretched beings who are doomed to be forever shut out from a Paradise for which they long,—a Paradise whose bright portals are guarded by the savage monster, Public Opinion, which ruthlessly denies the admission within its flowery precincts, of every poor daughter of Eve."

Mr. Tickels had listened with breathless attention to the words of the Duchess; he plainly saw that she was not to be subdued by *argument*. "Her only vulnerable point lies though the avenue of the passions," thought he—"for according to her own confession, she was intoxicated with rapture when encircled by my arms, and when receiving my ardent kisses; and only escaped the entire surrender of her person to me, by a powerful effort. My course, then, is plain—I must delicately and gradually venture on familiarities which are best calculated to arouse her sensibilities, without incurring her suspicions as to my ultimate object. I must—I shall succeed; for, by heaven! if I should fail to make this exquisite creature mine, I'll eat my own heart with vexatious disappointment!"

"My dear madam," said he, taking the unresisting hand of the Duchess in both of his, and gently pawing it in a manner that would have been disgusting to a spectator—"what can I say, after your candid avowal? Simply, that you are the most ingenuous, the most delightful creature in the world. I love you to distraction; and yet I will not urge you to depart from the course which you seem determined to pursue, though by adhering to that course you deprive me, as well as yourself, of the most exquisite delights this world can afford. Nevertheless, let us be friends, if we cannot be lovers. See, my hair is gray; I am old enough to be your father; will you not confer upon me a daughter's love? Ah, that bewitching smile is a token of assent. Thanks, sweet one; now, you know, a father should be the recipient of all his daughter's little joys and sorrows—he should be made acquainted with all her pretty plans and all her naughty wishes; is it not so, my charming daughter?[C] Again your soft smile answers, yes. And when the daughter thus bestows her confidence upon her father, she leans her head upon his bosom, and his protecting arm embraces her lovely waist—thus, as I now do yours. He places his venerated hand in her fair breast—thus—and feels the pulsations of her pure heart; ah! methinks this little heart of thine, sweet one, beats more violently than comports with its proper freedom from fond and gentle longings; thy father must reprove thee, thou delightful offender—yet he forgives thee with this loving kiss—nay, start not, for 'tis a father's privilege. How dewy are thy lips, my daughter, and thy breath is fragrant with the odor of a thousand flowers—'tis thy father tells thee so! Pretty flutterer, why dost thou tremble? I will not harm thee. Ah, is it so?—dost thou tremble with the bliss of being held in a father's arms, and pressed to his heart? Why doth this bosom heave—why do thine eyes sparkle as if with fire, and thy cheeks glow with the rosy hue of a ripe peach? What meaneth that longing, languishing, earnest, voluptuous look? Doth my daughter yearn after the soft joys of Venus?—Confess it, and I'll forgive thee; for thou art a passionate darling, and such desires as now swell within my breast become thee well, for they are nature's promptings, and enhance thy beauty. Ah, ha! that blush, glowing like a cloud at sunset, assures me that I am not mistaken. Yes, hide thy radiant face in my bosom, and let me gather thee closer to my heart—my life—my treasure! Let me no longer play the father; let me be thy lover—thy all—thy own Timothy—thy chosen Tickels! Ah, my bird, have I caught thee at last?—thou art mine—mine—mine—"

Every circumstance of position and the lady's compliance seemed about to confer upon Mr. Tickels the boon which he so eagerly desired, when at that critical moment the Duchess uttered a piercing scream, and pointed frantically upward to a large mirror that hung directly over the sofa upon which they were partially reclining; the old libertine glanced hurriedly up at the mirror, and to his horror he saw there reflected the figure of the Chevalier Duvall, standing in the centre of the room. He had entered abruptly and noiselessly, and was contemplating the scene before him with every appearance of astonishment and rage.

> [C] As an apology for the insertion of this silly, sickening rhapsody of the old libertine, the author begs to state that he introduced it, (as well as other speeches of a like character,) for the purpose of painting, in strong colors, the disgusting lechery of a man, whose primal passions had degraded him to the level of a brute. He would also assure the reader that the character of old Tickels is drawn from a living original, whose real name sounds very much like the curious cognomen that has been assigned him. It will readily be observed that during the entire scene between him and the Duchess, the latter makes him her complete tool—encouraging him to take the very liberties which she affects to resent, and even while declaring her firm intention of remaining virtuous, using language most calculated to inspire him with the thought of being able to enjoy her charms

in the end. Her object in all this will be shown towards the conclusion of the chapter. It has been the author's design to portray, in the character of the Duchess, an accomplished, artful, fascinating and totally depraved woman, possessing the beauty of an angel, and the heart of a devil—precisely such a one as could not fail to enslave and victimize such a sensual old wretch as Mr. Tickels; how far this design has been successful, the intelligent and discerning reader is left to judge. In the Chevalier Duvall will be recognized one of those splendid villains, whose superb rascality is cloaked beneath the mantle of a fine person, elegant address, and the assumption of every quality likely to interest and please the credulous people whom he *honors* with his patronising friendship.

The Duchess hid her face in her hands, and sobbed violently, as if overcome with shame and affright; while old Tickels, pale and trembling with fear, (for he was a most detestable coward,) fell upon his knees, and gazed upon the Chevalier with an expression of countenance that plainly indicated the terror which froze his blood, and rendered him speechless—for the position in which he and the Duchess had been detected, would, he well knew, admit of no explanation—no equivocation.

"God of heaven!" said Duvall, in a voice whose calmness rendered it doubly impressive and terrible—"am I the sport of some delusion—some conjuror's trick? Do I dream—or do these eyes actually behold that which appalls my soul? Speak, Duchess—for sister I will not call you—and you, white-faced craven—what is the meaning of this scene?"

But neither the Duchess nor Mr. Tickels could utter one word in reply.

"Damnation!" exclaimed the Chevalier, drawing a pistol from his pocket, and cocking it—"answer me, one of you, and that quickly, or there will be blood spilled here!"

This brought Mr. Tickels to his senses; he arose from his knees and stammered forth—

"My dear sir—don't shoot, for God's sake—put up that pistol, and I'll explain all. I—that is—you know, my dear Chevalier—as a man of the world—beautiful woman—strong temptation—"

"Hold, sir!" cried the Chevalier—"say no more, in that strain, or you die upon the instant. Duchess, tell me the meaning of all this."

The lady raised her tearful eyes imploringly to the stern face of her brother, and said, in a voice rendered indistinct by her sobs—

"Oh, brother! pardon your erring sister, who, in a moment of weakness, forgot her proud and unsullied name! You know the fire and passion of my nature; and you know the resolution with which I have heretofore struggled against it. I am inexperienced—unused to the ways of the world—unaccustomed to the artifices of wicked men. Debarred as I am from male society, what wonder that, in the company of a male, I should be overcome by the weakness of a woman's nature? Forgive me, Chevalier, I implore you—indeed, my honor is preserved; your timely intervention prevented the consummation of my ruin."

"Sister," rejoined Duvall, gazing at her with a softened aspect—"I *do* forgive you, your honor being still undefiled; I know the power of your passions, notwithstanding your many excellent qualities; and I can scarcely wonder at your momentary weakness, when an accomplished villain tempts you to ruin. Hereafter, dear sister, govern those unruly passions with a rod of iron; remember the grandeur of our ancestral house and name, and let that remembrance be your safeguard.—As for you, sir," continued the Chevalier, turning savagely towards Mr. Tickels, while his magnificent features grew dark with terrible rage—"as for you, sir, you have betrayed my confidence and abused my hospitality; I introduced you into this house, supposing you to be a man of honor and a friend. You have attempted the seduction of my sister; you have basely tried to take advantage of the weakness of an inexperienced and unsuspecting woman; but more than all this, sir—and my blood boils with fury at the thought!—you would have tarnished the unstained name and honor of a kingly race! Look you, sir, these wrongs demand instant reparation—one or both of us must die. Here are two pistols; take your choice; place yourself at the distance of six paces from me, and let impartial Fate decide the issue!"

"But, my dear sir," cried the old villain, almost beside himself with terror—"I can't—I don't want to be killed—my God, sir, I never fired a pistol in all my life. Can't we settle this matter in some other way? Will not *money*—"

"Money!" exclaimed me Chevalier, scornfully—"fool, can money heal a wounded honor, or wipe away the odium of your insults? Choose your weapon, sir!"

"Mercy—mercy!" cried the dastard, falling on his knees before his stern antagonist—"I am rich, let me depart in safety, and I'll give you a cheque for a hundred—"

The Chevalier cocked a pistol.

"Five hundred—," groaned Tickels.

The pistol was raised, and pointed at his head.

"A thousand dollars!" yelled the victim, his face streaming with a cold perspiration, his hair bristling, and his teeth chattering with fright.

The Chevalier paused, and said, after a few moments' reflection—

"After all, to make such men as you disgorge a portion of their wealth, is a punishment as severe as any that I can inflict upon you. You are a coward and dare not fight; I wish not to murder you in cold blood. I will content myself with exposing your infamous conduct to the world—publishing your rascality in every newspaper, and you will be kicked like a dog from all decent society; this will I do, unless you immediately fill me out a cheque for the sum of five thousand dollars."

"Five thousand devils!" growled Tickels, gaining courage as he believed his life to be in no imminent danger—"what! five thousand dollars for only having kissed and toyed a little with a pretty woman, without having reaped any substantial benefit? No, no, my friend—you can't come it; you are, to use a vulgar phrase, cutting it rather fat; I'm not so precious green as you think. I don't mind giving you a couple of hundred, or so, for what fun I've had, but five thousand—whew! rather a high price for the amusement, considering what a remarkably free-and-easy lady your sister is!"

"No more of this!" thundered the Chevalier, in a tone that made Mr. Tickels leap two feet into the air—"instantly give me a cheque for the sum that I demand, or by my royal grandfather's beard, (an oath I dare not break,) I'll blow your head into fragments!—Look at that clock; it now lacks one minute of the hour; that minute I give you to decide; if, at the expiration of that period, you do not consent to do as I request, you die!"

The muzzle of the pistol was placed in very close proximity to the victim's head; there was no alternative—life was exceedingly sweet to Mr. Tickels, although the wickedness of half a century rested heavily on his soul; in a few seconds more, unless he consented to give up a portion of his basely acquired wealth, he had every reason to fear that soul would be ushered into a dark and unfathomable eternity. No wonder, then, that he tremulously said—

"Put up your weapon; I will do as you require."

Writing materials were soon brought, and in a few minutes the Chevalier was the possessor of a cheque on a State street bank, bearing the substantial autograph of Timothy Tickels.

"Now, sir," said Duvall, depositing the valuable document in his pocket-book—"you are at liberty to depart. I am confident that you will, for your own sake, keep this affair a profound secret; and so far as myself and much-injured sister are concerned, you may rest assured that nothing shall ever be said calculated to compromise your reputation. I cannot avoid expressing my regret that a man of your advanced age, and high standing in society, should descend so low as to manifest such base and grovelling sensuality—such unprincipled libertinism—especially towards a lady who has heretofore regarded you as a friend. Go, sir, and seek some other victim, if you will—but confine your amours to your own class, and do not again aspire to the favors of a lady in whose veins flows the noblest blood of France!"

Mr. Tickels took his leave of the indignant brother and his much-injured sister, with a very ill grace; and bent his steps towards his own house, grinding his teeth with impotent rage. The loss of his money, and the mortifying disappointment he had experienced, rendered him furious, and he muttered as he strode thro' the streets with hasty and irregular steps—

"Eternal curse on my ill fortune! Five thousand dollars gone at one fell swoop—but hah! the money's nothing, when I think of my being cheated out of the enjoyment of such celestial charms as those possessed by that splendid enchantress!—At the very critical moment—when she lay panting and unresisting in my arms—with all her glorious beauties spread out before me, like the delicious materials of a dainty feast—just as the cup of joy was raised to my eager lips, and I was about to quaff its bewildering contents, to be balked by the unexpected entrance of that accused Chevalier. Confusion!—I shall go mad with vexation. **** Well, 'tis of no use to grumble about what can't be helped; let me rather turn my attention to future joys, concerning which there can be no disappointment. My plans are all arranged; in a few days my pretty Fanny Aubrey will be an inmate of the luxurious "Chambers of Love." Ha, ha! *that* thought almost reconciles me to the loss of the Duchess—though, egad! *she* is a luscious piece, all fire, all sentiment, all enthusiasm! But oh! five thousand dollars, five thousand dollars! *** But let me see: where is the infernal trap of that scoundrel, *Jew Mike*, whom Sow Nance recommended as a fellow well qualified to abduct my pretty Fanny, and convey her to the "Chambers?" Ah, good; his address is in my memorandum book: *'Inquire for the Pig Pen, No.—Ann street, any night after midnight.'* Ugh! I don't like this venturing among cut-throats and thieves, at such untimely hours; but nothing risk, nothing have; and anything for love!"

The reader's attention is now summoned to the scene which transpired between the Chevalier and the Duchess, immediately after the departure of Mr. Tickels from the house.

The Duchess, who had been sitting upon the sofa, bathed in tears and sobbing as if her heart would break, jumped up, bounded across the carpet in a series of graceful pirouettes, and then, throwing herself upon the floor, indulged in a peal of silvery laughter that made the room fairly echo, exclaiming—

"What a d——d old fool that man is! Oh, I shall die—I shall positively suffocate with mirth!"

The Chevalier, throwing aside every appearance of indignation and dignity, placed himself in that humorous and rather vulgar position, sometimes adopted by jocose youths, who wish to intimate to their friends the fact that any individual has been most egregiously "sucked in." Fearing that the uninitiated may not readily comprehend this pantomimic witticism, we may as well state, for their enlightenment, that it is accomplished by applying the thumb to the tip of the nose, and executing a series of gyrations with the open hand; the whole affair being a very playful and ingenious invention, much practised by newsboys, cabmen, second-hand clothes dealers, and sporting gentlemen.

"A cool five thousand!" shouted the Chevalier, abandoning this comic picture, and "squaring off" at his reflection in the mirror, in the most approved style of the pugilistic art—as if he were about to give himself a "punch in the head," for being such a funny, clever dog; "bravo! I'll go and get the cheque cashed at once; and then hurrah for a brilliant season of glorious dissipation! But, my Duchess, how the devil did you mange to get the old fool so infatuated—so crazy with passion? for I stood over ten minutes looking at both of you through the key-hole, before I entered the room, and I never before saw a man act so extravagantly ludicrous; it was only with extreme difficulty that I could keep myself from laughing outright. And you, witch that you are, looked as if you were panting and dying with amorous desires. By my soul, 'twas admirably done!"

The Duchess smiled with gratification at the praise; and arising from the carpet, on which she had been literally *rolling* in the excess of her mirth, threw herself upon the sofa in an attitude of voluptuous abandonment; and while complacently viewing her matchless leg, she said—

"For your especial entertainment, my Chevalier, I will relate all that transpired between me and the old goat, after your departure. At first, he assailed me with a profusion of silly, sickening compliments on my beauty; I blushed, (you know how well I *can* blush, when I try,) and assured him that his praises were divine—so eloquent, so elegantly conveyed—and yet I thought them intolerably stupid. Then I gave him my hand to kiss; and its contact with his lips made him as amorous as I could possibly desire. He knelt at my feet; then arose, apologizing for his rudeness. I threw all my powers of fascination into my looks, and permitted him to take a seat by my side, on the sofa. At first, he sat apart from me; but at last, gaining courage, he moved close to me, and gently placed his arm around my waist; of course, I did not repulse him. With secret joy I observed the eagerness with which he regarded such parts of my person as were exposed—and I took good care to reveal it liberally; how the odious old wretch gloated upon this bust, which you, my Chevalier, pronounce so charming! At last, he kissed me—ugh! how horribly the old creature's breath smelt! But I pretended to be more pleased than angry; and from my lips his nauseous mouth wandered to my neck, my shoulders, my bosom. I fairly shuddered as he besmeared me with his disgusting kisses; and thinking that he had gone far enough, for that time, I burst from his embrace, and reproached him (but not too severely,) for his rude behavior—taking good care, however, to fan his passions into a still fiercer flame, by telling him that my reason for particularly dreading such familiarities, was, that they had a tendency to excite my own desires to a degree that was dangerous to my honor. As I foresaw, this artful assurance was received by him with ill-concealed delight. He begged my pardon; it is needless to say, I forgave him, and suffered him to resume his seat at my side, on condition that he would take no further liberties, knowing very well that he could not long keep his promise. Then came more compliments; I sang and played for him, and he was beyond measure delighted. After a short conversation on the secluded manner in which I lived, and the loneliness which I felt, I confessed to him that I was half in love with him; while at the same time I thought him the most disgusting old brute in existence. In return for my pleasing lie, he pressed my hand fervently, and requested me to relate to him the story of my life, from "my own rosy lips," as he said. My Chevalier, you know what splendid powers of imagination, and what a rich, prolific fancy I possess; and well I may—for am I not a leading contributor to a fashionable ladies' magazine, besides being the authoress of "Confessions of a Voluptuous Young Lady of High Rank," and also the editress of the last edition of the "Memoirs of Miss Frances Hill?" Well, I entertained my aged admirer with a pretty little impromptu "romance," "got up expressly for the occasion," as the playbills have it; and he religiously believed every word of it—though, of course, it contained not one single word of truth in it. I told him that *my brother* and myself—ha, ha!—were the children of some Duke Thingumby, (whose name I have forgotten already,) who was one of the greatest nobles in France; yes, faith—our venerable papa had royal blood in his veins, while our mamma, bless her dear soul, was 'closely allied to several of the most aristocratic families in the kingdom.' Then I trumped up a cock-and-bull story about papa killing mamma in a fit of jealousy, having caught her in a naughty fix with the young Count Somebody-or-other, whom he also slew, and then, to wind up the fun, went to his own chamber and shot himself—great booby as he was! Next, the notary who had charge of our princely fortune, "stepped out," as they say, and left us, poor orphans, without the price of a penny roll. I was intensely virtuous, of course, resisted a hundred tempting offers to become the kept mistress of men of wealth and rank—we came to America, and settled in Boston, where you now obtain for us a comfortable subsistence by privately teaching the use of the small sword. Ah, my Chevalier, wasn't that brought in well? Then I went on to lament that my passions were so fiery that I could not enjoy the society of an agreeable man without danger to my honor; and concluded my story by hinting to Mr. Tickels that my virtue had never been in such peril, as when his arms had embraced me—for, said I, my senses were fast becoming intoxicated; and in a few moments more I should have been your victim, had I not, by a powerful effort, escaped from the sweet delirium which was stealing over my soul. Thus you will see, Chevalier, that my story and its accompanying remarks were both judicious and appropriate; my victim manifested the most intense interest during the recital, and I could plainly perceive the exciting effect which the concluding words of my narrative had upon him.

> "My story being done,
> He gave me for my pains a world of sighs."

"After the completion of my delightful little romance," continued the Duchess, "the venerable goat attempted to subdue me by the force of *argument*; and, to do him justice, I must say that his philosophy, if not very rational, was at least very profound. He went over the entire field of moral subtleties, and proved himself an excellent sophist. He argued that as nature had given me passions, I was justified in gratifying them, despite the opinions of the world and the prohibitions of decent society. Much more he said that I have forgotten; but the drift of his remarks was, that as I had admitted him to be the most charming and agreeable person in the world, I could not do a better thing than to throw myself into his arms, and enjoy with him, as he said, 'the rightful inheritance of every man and every woman on the face of the earth.'"

"In reply to his specious reasoning, I assured him that I couldn't think of complying with his wishes, as I should thereby lose my reputation and position in society, as a lady—which was, I added, the only consideration that restrained me from testing those joys which he had so eloquently depicted; for as to any scruples, moral or religious, I had none whatever. Then I congratulated him on his happiness in belonging to a sex having the privilege of amative delights, with almost perfect impunity; and deplored my own hard fate—'for', said I, 'am I not a woman, and are not women sternly prohibited from tasting the joys of love unsanctioned by the empty forms of matrimony, under pain of having their names and characters forever blasted and disgraced?'

"Well, my Chevalier, the old wretch, seeing that he was not likely to accomplish his object by argument, adopted a new plan. Instantly, he dropped the lover, and became the fond and doting father, in which sacred capacity he proceeded to take liberties to which his former familiarities were as nothing. He began by reminding me of his gray hair and advanced age; then he asked permission to regard me as a daughter, to which I made no objection, as I wished to see how far he would operate during the personation of that character—though I shrewdly suspected that his actions would be anything but fatherly. Therefore, when he again clasped my waist, and made me lean against him, I did not repulse him, for his conduct was in furtherance of *our* plans; and I also permitted him, (though with extreme disgust on my part,) to toy with my breasts, and kiss me again and again, all of which he did under cover of his holy privileges as a father! The moment had then arrived for *me* to play *my* part; and though the old rascal's conduct and person were loathsome to me in the extreme, I affected all the languor, flutter, and ardor of passionate longings; which he perceived with the most extravagant demonstrations of delight—"

"I know all the rest," interrupted the Chevalier, almost suffocated with laughter, in which the merry Duchess joined him—"I applied my eye to the key-hole just at that moment, and saw the old goat, as you properly term him, hugging you with the ferocity of a bear; I heard him say—'Let me no longer play the father; let me be thy lover—thy all—thy own Timothy—thy chosen Tickels!' Ha, ha, ha! was anything so richly ludicrous. And, by Jove, how admirably you acted, my Duchess! You appeared absolutely dying with rapture—your eyes seemed to express a thousand soft wishes—your face glowed as if with the heat of languishing desire; how wildly you seemed to abandon your person to his lascivious embraces! and yet I know the disgust which you must have felt towards him, at that very moment; for he was anything but a comely object, with his gray hair disordered, his bloated countenance red as fire, and his dress indecently disarranged. At that moment I noiselessly stole into the room; and just at the very instant when the old fool thought himself sure of his prey, you screamed, and pointed to my reflection in the mirror. The result was precisely as I expected; too cowardly to fight, afraid of his life, and anxious to preserve his reputation, he preferred giving me the handsome sum of five thousand dollars—which money we very much needed, and which will last us a long time, provided we exercise a reasonable degree of economy. That last five hundred, which we extracted from the parson, lasted us but little over a month; let us be more discreet hereafter, my Duchess—we may live splendidly, but not extravagantly; for old age will come on us by-and-by, and your beauty will fade—then what is to become of us, unless we have a snug competency in reserve? And really, my dear, you must curtail your personal expenditures; you recollect but a week ago you gave two hundred dollars for that diamond coronet you have on—and you are constantly purchasing costly dresses and superb shawls. Do you not observe the plainness of my attire? Believe me, an elegant simplicity of dress is far more attractive to men of taste, than gaudy apparel can possibly be."

"Have you done sermonizing?" cried the Duchess, good-humoredly—"really, you would make an admirable parson; and a far better one, I am sure, than the reverend gentleman whom we wheedled out of the five hundred dollars. But go at once and get the cheque cashed; you shall give me exactly one half, and we both shall have the privilege of expending our several portions as we choose."

"Agreed," said the Chevalier,—"but I have a little business to transact in my *workshop*, before I go to the bank. What are you laughing at?"

"Oh," answered the Duchess—"I cannot help thinking of that amusing old goat, Mr. Tickels. The recollection of that man will certainly kill me! The idea of your passing me off as your sister was so rich; he little suspected that for years we have been tender lovers and co-partners in the business of fleecing amorous gentlemen out of their money. And then to represent myself as the daughter of a French nobleman!—Why, my father gained a very pretty living by going around the streets with a hand-organ, on which he played with exquisite skill, and was accompanied in his perambulations by a darling little monkey named Jacko—poor Jacko! he came to his death by being choked with a roasted potato. My mother, rest her soul! was an excellent washerwoman, but her unfortunate fondness for strong drink resulted in her being provided with bed and board in the alms house, in which excellent institution she died, having first conferred upon the world the benefit of bringing me into existence; therefore, instead of having first seen the light within the marble walls of a French palace, I drew my first breath in the sick ward of a pauper's home. At ten years of age I was a *ballet girl* at the theatre; at fourteen, my Chevalier, it was my good fortune to meet you; you initiated me, not only into the mysteries of love, but into the art of making money with far greater facility than as a *figurante* in the opera.

You christened me 'Duchess,'—took the title of 'Chevalier,' and together we have led a life of profit, of pleasure, and of charming variety."

"And I," rejoined the Chevalier, "can boast of a parentage as distinguished as your own. My father was an English thief and pickpocket; he took pains to teach me the science of his profession, and I will venture to affirm that I can remove a gentleman's watch or pocket-book as gracefully as could my venerated sire himself, whose career was rather abruptly terminated one fine morning in consequence of a temporary valet having tied his neckcloth too tightly: he was hung in front of Newgate jail, for a highway robbery, in which he acquired but little glory and less profit,—for he only shot an old woman's poodle dog, and stole a leather purse full of halfpence. My mother was a very pretty waiting woman at an ordinary tavern; one night she abruptly stepped out and sailed for America, carrying with her my unfinished self, and the silver spoons. I saw you—admired you—made you my mistress, and partner in business, the profitable nature of which is proved by our being now possessed of the very pretty sum of five thousand dollars, the result of three hours' operation."

"You have yet one grand stroke of art to accomplish, which will place us both on the very pinnacle of fortune," said the Duchess. "I allude, of course, to your approaching marriage with Miss Alice Goldworthy."

The Chevalier's brow darkened, and his handsome features assumed an expression of uneasiness.

"That," said he, "is the only business in which I ever faltered. Poor young lady! she is so good, so pure, so confidingly affectionate, that my heart sinks within me when I think of the ruin which her marriage with me will bring upon her. When I gaze into her lovely countenance, and hear the tones of her gentle voice, remorse for the wrong that I contemplate towards her, strikes me to the soul, and I feel that I am a wretch indeed."

"Pooh!" exclaimed the Duchess, her lips curling with disdain—"you grow very sentimental indeed! Perhaps you really *love* this girl?"

"No, Duchess, no—but I pity her; a devil cannot love an angel. There was a time when my soul was unstained with guilt or crime—then might I have aspired to the bliss of loving such a divine creature as Alice; but now—villain as I am there can be no sympathy between my heart and hers. Well, well—the die is cast; I will wed her, for I covet the splendid fortune which she will inherit on the death of her father. You know that the wedding day will soon arrive; but how I dread its approach! for I fear that ere I can embrace my bride within the sacred nuptial couch, she will discover that which I can never remove or entirely conceal—that *fatal mark*, the brand of crime, which I carry upon my person. She loves me; but her love would be changed to hate, were she to see that horrid emblem of guilt."

"You must conceal it from her view," rejoined the Duchess, shuddering—"or it will spoil all. The marriage would be annulled by the discovery of that detestable mark."

"Let us trust to fortune," said the Chevalier.—"I must leave you now, and shut myself up for an hour or so in my *workshop*. Afterwards, I shall go and convert the cheque into substantial cash."

Duvall left the room, and ascended to the highest story in the building. Here he entered a small apartment, which contained many curious and remarkable things. A small printing press stood in one corner; in another was a pile of paper, and other materials; tools of almost every description lay scattered about, among which were the necessary implements for robbery and burglary. An experienced police officer would have instantly pronounced the place a secret den for the printing of counterfeit bank-notes—and so it was. The gallant Chevalier was the most expert and dangerous counterfeiter in the country.

Seating himself at a trunk, on which stood writing materials, he drew forth the cheque which Mr. Tickels had given him. Having examined it long and narrowly, he took a pen and paper, and wrote an exact copy of it; this he did so admirably, that Mr. Tickels himself would have been puzzled to point out the original and genuine cheque which he had written.

"This will do," said the Chevalier, communing with himself—"to-day I will draw five thousand dollars; and within a week I will *send* and draw five thousand more; and it shall be done so adroitly, that I will never be suspected. Hurrah! Chevalier Duvall, thy star is on the ascendant!"

That afternoon the gentleman presented the cheque at the bank; it was promptly paid, and he returned to the Duchess, with whom he celebrated the brilliant success of the operation, by a magnificent supper.

Chapter VI
The Stolen Package.—The Midnight Outrage.—The Marriage, and Awful Discovery

A very merry party were assembled in the elegant parlor of Mr. Goldworthy's superb mansion in Howard street about two weeks after the events described in the last chapter. There was Fanny Aubrey herself, looking prettier than ever, with her splendid hair tastefully braided, her graceful, *petite* form set off to advantage by an elegant dress, and her lovely countenance radiant with the hues of health and happiness. Then there was her friend and benefactress, Miss Alice, looking very beautiful, her face constantly changing from smiles to blushes—for the next day was to witness her marriage with the Chevalier Duvall. At her side was seated her lover and affianced husband, his dark, handsome features lighted up with an expression of proud triumph, almost amounting to scorn. Then there was Corporal Grimsby, very shabby, very sarcastic, and very droll; near him sat the Honorable Timothy Tickels, wearing upon his sensual countenance a look of uneasiness, and occasionally betraying a degree of nervous agitation that indicated a mind ill at ease. At intervals he would glance suspiciously and stealthily at the Chevalier—for that was their first meeting since his scandalous adventure with the Duchess, and he was not without a fear that he might be exposed, in the presence of that very respectable company, in which case his reputation would be forever ruined; but his fears were groundless—the Chevalier had not the remotest idea of exposing him, having his own reasons for keeping the affair profoundly secret; and he saluted and conversed with Mr. Tickels with as much composure and politeness as though nothing had ever happened to disturb the harmony of their friendship. Mr. Goldworthy himself was present, and also a nephew of his—a handsome youth of nineteen, named Clarence Argyle; he was studying the profession of medicine at a Southern University, and was on a visit at his uncle's house. It was evident, by the assiduity of his attentions to Fanny Aubrey, that the mental and personal charms of the fair maid were not without their effect upon him; and it was equally evident by the pleased smile with which she listened to his entertaining conversation—addressed to *her* ear alone—that the agreeable young stranger had impressed her mind by no means unfavorably. Fanny's brother, Charles, completed the party.

It will be necessary to explain here, that the old Corporal had never exposed the rascally conduct of Mr. Tickels towards Fanny, in consequence of the young lady's having earnestly entreated him not to do so. He had never before met the old libertine at the house of Mr. Goldworthy; and (until informed of the fact by Fanny,) was ignorant that he (Tickels) was in the habit of visiting there, as a friend of the family. He treated him with coldness and reserve; but otherwise gave no indication of the contempt which he felt for the unprincipled old wretch.

As Mr. Goldworthy surveyed, with a smiling aspect, the sociable group which surrounded him, little did he suspect that the man who on the morrow was to become his son-in-law—who was to lead to the altar his only child, that pure and gentle girl—little, we say, did he suspect that the Chevalier Duvall was in reality a branded villain of the blackest dye—a man whose soul was stained by the commission of almost every crime on the dark catalogue of guilt. And as little did he think that his warm political and personal friend, the Honorable Timothy Tickels—the man of ample wealth, of unbounded influence, of exalted reputation—was at heart an abandoned and licentious scoundrel, who had basely tried to accomplish the ruin of a poor orphan girl, and was even at that very moment gloating over an infernal plan which he had formed, for getting her completely in his power, where no human aid was likely to reach her.

"To-morrow, my Alice," whispered the Chevalier in the ear of the blushing object of his villainous designs—"to-morrow, thou are mine! Oh, the devotion of a life-time shall atone to you for the sacrifice you make, in wedding an unknown stranger, whose birth and fortunes are shrouded in a veil of mystery."

"Thy birth and fortunes are nothing to me," responded Alice, softly, as a tear of happiness trembled in her eyes—"so long as thy heart is faithful and true."

What wonder that the Chevalier's false heart grew cold in his breast, at the simple words of the confiding, gentle, unsuspecting creature whom he designed to ruin? But still he hesitated not; "her father's gold is the glittering prize which I shall gain by this marriage," thought he; and the vile, sordid thought stimulated him on, despite the remonstrances of his better nature.

"When I return to the University, we will write to each other often, will we not?" said Clarence Argyle to Fanny, in a tone that could not be overheard by the others of the party; and the fair girl yielded a blushing consent to the proposal, so congenial to her own inclination. The whisper and the blush were both observed by old Tickels, who said to himself—

"Humph! 'tis easy to see that those two unfledged Cupids are already over head and ears in love with each other. Have a care, Master Argyle—thy pretty mistress may be lost to thee to-morrow; go back to thy books and thy studies—for she is not for thee. Ah, the devil! I like not the look which that impertinent old fellow, who calls himself Corporal Grimsby, fastens upon me—it seems as if he read the secret thoughts of my soul! He has once already snatched from my grasp my destined prey; let him beware how he interferes a second time, for Jew Mike is in my employ, and his knife is sharp and his aim sure!"

"That d——d scoundrel, Tickels, meditates mischief, I am convinced," thought the Corporal, whose keen and penetrating gaze had been for some time riveted upon the old libertine—"and I feel convinced that my pretty Fanny is the object of his secret machinations. Beware, old Judas Iscariot!—you'll not get off so easy the next time I catch you at your tricks."

"And so, my dear Mr. Tickels, you are again a candidate for Congress," remarked Mr. Goldworthy, during a pause in the conversation.

"I again have that distinguished honor," was the pompous reply. "My party stands in great need of my services and influence in the House at the present crisis."

"No doubt," dryly observed the Corporal—"I would suggest that your first public act be the introduction of a bill for the punishment of seduction, and the protection of poor orphan girls."

Mr. Tickels writhed beneath the sarcasm, and turned deadly pale, although he and his tormentor were the only persons present who comprehended the secret meaning of the words—for Fanny was too much engrossed in conversation with Argyle, to heed the remark.

"And, my good sir," rejoined the Chevalier, who was resolved to improve so good an opportunity to wound the old reprobate to the quick, (although he was ignorant of the application of the Corporal's words,)—"do not, I beseech you, neglect to insert a clause in your bill, providing also for the punishment of those respectable old wretches who bring ruin and disgrace upon families, by the seduction of wives—of daughters—or of *sisters*! I confess myself interested in the passage of such an act, in consequence of a wealthy old scoundrel having once dared to insult grievously a near female relative of mine. The name of this old wretch—"

Tickels cast an imploring look at the Chevalier, and the latter was silent—but upon his lips remained an expression of withering scorn;

for villain as he himself was, he detested the other for his consummate hypocrisy. The vicious frequently hate others for possessing the same evil qualities that characterise themselves. The character of the Chevalier was doubtless hypocritical in its nature; but *his* hypocrisy was, in our opinion, far less contemptible than that of Tickels; the former was a hypocrite for pecuniary gain; the latter, for the gratification of the basest and most grovelling propensities that can disgrace humanity.

"Gentlemen—gentlemen!" cried Mr. Goldworthy, amazed at the turn which the conversation had taken, and comprehending neither of the allusions—"I beg you to remember that there are ladies present."

"Blood and bayonets!" exclaimed the Corporal—"you are right: I forgot the ladies, my worthy host, and crave your pardon and theirs, for my indiscreet (though I must say, *devilish appropriate*) remarks!"

The Chevalier also apologized, though with less circumlocution than the worthy Corporal; and nothing further occurred to disturb either the harmony of the company, or the equanimity of Mr. Tickels, until Mr. Goldworthy, with a countenance full of astonishment and alarm, announced to his guests that he had, during the evening, lost from his pocket a package of banknotes and valuable papers, amounting to some thousands of dollars, which he had procured for investment the following day in an extensive mercantile speculation—for although retired from active business, he still frequently ventured large sums in operations which were generally successful.

For half an hour previous to making his fearful discovery, he had been in private and earnest conversation with the Chevalier, concerning some arrangements relative to the approaching marriage.

"It is indeed astonishing—what can have become of it?" cried the old gentleman, searching every pocket in vain for the missing package. "I am certain that 'twas safely in my possession scarce one hour ago," continued he; and summoning a couple of servants, he commanded a diligent search to be made in every part of the room—but still in vain; no package was to be found.

Everybody present, with but one exception, expressed their concern and astonishment; that exception was Fanny Aubrey; she was much agitated, and pale as death.

It was suggested by the Chevalier and several others, that he must have dropped the package in the street, as it could not be found in the house. In reply to this, Mr. Goldworthy said—

"No, no, my friend—I will swear that I lost it in this very room, within an hour. Plague on it! what particularly vexes me, is, that it comprised all my present available capital—and to have it disappear in such a d——d unaccountable, mysterious manner! Why, curse it," cried the old gentleman, getting more and more angry—"if I didn't know the thing to be impossible, I should suspect that there was an accomplished pickpocket in the room!"

"So should I," dryly observed the Corporal; and so said the Hon. Mr. Tickels, also.

The Chevalier arose, and said, with calm dignity—

"Gentlemen, I conceive that an insinuation has been made, derogatory to our honor. Mr. Goldworthy, your words indirectly imply a suspicion; I must request you, sir, to explain your words, and to state distinctly whether or no you suppose that any person present has robbed you. I also suggest that all here be carefully searched."

"Good heavens, my dear Chevalier!" cried Mr. Goldworthy, much excited—"can you think for a moment that I suspect you or these gentlemen, of an act so base and contemptible? Pardon my hasty words; vexation at my great loss (a serious one, I assure you,) for a moment overcame my temper. Let the package go to the devil, sooner than its loss should occasion the least uneasiness to any of us. Come, my dear friends, let's say no more about it."

Harmony was once more restored; but still Fanny Aubrey looked so pale and agitated, that Miss Alice, crossing over to where she sat, anxiously inquired if she were unwell? The poor girl essayed to reply, but could not; it was evident to her friend, that she was struggling with feelings of the most painful nature. She pressed Alice's hand, burst into tears, and abruptly left the room.

"The poor girl is either very unwell, or very much troubled about something," whispered Alice to her cousin Clarence—"I will go and comfort her;" and having made her excuses to the company, she left the room, and followed Fanny to her chamber.

Her departure was the signal for the guests to take their leave of their worthy host. Mr. Goldworthy warmly pressed the Chevalier's hand at parting, and said to him—

"To-morrow, my dear sir, you will be my son-in-law. Be kind to my Alice, she is a good girl, and worthy of you. God bless you both! I did intend to advance you a sum of money, sufficient to enable you to begin housekeeping in handsome style; but the loss of that large sum of money to-night will, I fear, place it out of my power to assist you much, at present. However, I shall endeavor to raise a respectable sum for you, in the course of a few days. Meantime, you and Alice must be my guests; and I am not sure but that I shall insist upon your continually residing beneath my roof—

for I am a lonely old man, and so accustomed to the kind attentions and sweet society of my only daughter, that to part with her would deprive me of half my earthly joys. Farewell—may you and her be happy together!"

Tears stood in the eyes of the good old man, as he uttered these words; and again the conscience of the Chevalier upbraided him for his contemplated villainy—but still he paused not nor faltered in carrying out his diabolical schemes.

Meanwhile, the following scene occurred in Fanny's chamber, to which Alice had repaired for the purpose of ascertaining the cause of the young girl's agitation and tears.

"What is the matter, my dear sister? For such I will call you," said Alice, clasping her arms around the weeping girl, who had thrown herself upon the bed without undressing.

"Oh, my friend, my benefactress!" cried Fanny—"how can I help feeling so distressed, when I know that your happiness is about to be destroyed forever?"

"My happiness destroyed!" cried Alice, surprised and alarmed—"what mean you! Do you allude to my marriage to-morrow with the Chevalier Duvall? Yes, I see you do. Silly girl, that marriage will render me the happiest of women; what reason have you for supposing otherwise? The Chevalier loves me, and I sincerely reciprocate his affection; so dry your tears, for you know you are to be bridesmaid, and smiles better become you than tears."

These words were spoken in the kindest and gentlest tone; but Fanny exclaimed—

"Miss Alice, you are cruelly deceived in that man."

"Deceived!" cried the young lady—"what mystery is hidden in your words? Oh, if you love me, Fanny—and you have often told me that you did—instantly explain the meaning of your dreadful declaration."

"Listen to me, Miss Alice," said Fanny, with a calmness that strangely contrasted with her previous agitation—"and I will tell you plainly what I have seen, and what I think. To you I owe everything: the comforts of a home, the kindness of a friend, and the benefits of a superior education, now enjoyed by my brother and myself—two poor orphans, who, but for your benevolence, would be dependent upon the world's cold charity. My gratitude I can never express; my heart alone can feel it—but oh! believe me, I would gladly lay down my life to promote your happiness. How, then, can I see future years of misery awaiting you, without tears of anguish—

without feeling an intense anxiety to preserve you from a fate ten times worse than death?"

"Do not interrupt me, I pray you," continued Fanny, seeing that Alice was about to speak—"To-morrow you are engaged to be married to the man calling himself the Chevalier Duvall. When I first saw him, I was struck with his beauty and accomplishments—his brilliant wit, and graceful manners; and when, in sisterly confidence, you informed me that he was your affianced husband, you know how warmly I congratulated you on having won the affections of a man who, as I then believed, was in every way calculated to make you happy.

"Alice, I tell you that man is a villain!" cried Fanny, with startling emphasis—"I saw him pick your father's pocket of the money that was lost; yes, I alone saw him do it; *that* was the cause of my agitation and tears. Do not marry him, for he is a robber and a scoundrel!"

"Say no more, Miss Aubrey," said Alice, rising with an air of cold dignity, which plainly indicated her entire disbelief of the statement she had just heard—"Say no more: you have mistaken your position, when you seek to prejudice me against a gentleman whom I am so soon to call my husband. Nay, not a word more—I will not listen to you. The Chevalier Duvall is the very soul of honor; and to accuse *him*—how can I say it?— of the crime of *theft*, is so preposterous that it would be ludicrous under any other circumstances. Fanny, I can scarcely believe that you have been actuated by *jealousy* in telling this dreadful story; I will try to think that your eyes deceived you, and that you really *thought* that you saw the Chevalier do as you have said. But oh! how mistaken you are, unhappy girl! when you impute such a crime to one of the noblest and best of men."

"But, Miss Alice," cried Fanny, almost angrily—for she was certain of the truth of her statement—"I tell you that I am not mistaken; I saw—"

"Silence, I entreat—I command you!" cried the young lady, now thoroughly indignant at the disgraceful accusation which had been brought against her lover—"speak not another word to me on this odious subject, or you forfeit my friendship forever. Good night; learn in future to be more discreet."

So saying, Alice left the unhappy young girl to her bitter tears. Soon wearied nature asserted her rights, and she sobbed herself to sleep. But her slumbers were disturbed by hideous dreams: in fancy she again saw the magnificent Chevalier dexterously abstract the package of money from Mr. Goldworthy's pocket—then she thought that the brilliant stranger stood over her, and surveyed her with an expression of fearful menace. The scene again changed; she was alone, in a vast and splendid apartment, reclining upon a sumptuous couch; delicious music, from invisible minstrels, soothed her soul into a sort of dreamy and voluptuous trance; an unearthly happiness filled her heart—her senses were intoxicated with delight. Suddenly, in the dim distance, she saw a Hideous Object, and the blood went tingling through her veins with terror; it had the form of a gigantic reptile; slowly it crawled towards the couch on which she lay; dim grew the light from the sparkling chandeliers—heavy grew the air with noxious odors; the Hideous Object crouched beneath the bed; she heard its deep breathing—its heavy sighs; then it reared its awful form above her, and then approached its ghastly head to hers; she felt its foul breath upon her cheek— its green dragon-like eyes penetrated her soul, and made her brain dizzy—it fanned her by the flapping of its mighty wings. It breathed into her ear vile whispers, tempting her to crime. It placed its huge vulture's claw upon her heart, as if to tear it from her breast. She awoke.

Gracious heavens! there—there—at her bed-side, stood a human form, its countenance dark and threatening—the savage features almost totally concealed by masses of black and shaggy hair. A rough, hard hand rested upon her breast, and a pair of fierce, cruel eyes struck terror to her soul.

She uttered one piercing scream, and fainted. The report of a pistol was heard; then hasty footsteps descended the stair-case; the hall was rapidly traversed—the street door was opened and shut with a loud noise—and all was still.

In a few minutes the affrightened inmates of the mansion, half dressed, were hastening to the scene of the late tumult; Mr. Goldworthy and his daughter Alice were among them. What was the astonishment and dismay of the startled group, on discovering that Fanny Aubrey was nowhere to be found, while at her chamber door, wounded and bleeding, lay the insensible form of Clarence Argyle!

They raised the young gentleman, and placed him upon the bed; a physician, who fortunately resided next door, and was almost instantly upon the spot, pronounced the wound severe, but not dangerous. He had been shot in the breast; the ball was with some difficulty extracted, and the patient rendered as comfortable as possible.

But where was the clue to all this fearful mystery? What had become of Fanny Aubrey? Who had dared to enter that house at midnight, and after nearly murdering one of the inmates, carry off a young lady? What was the *object* of the perpetrator of the outrage? These were the questions uttered by everybody present; but no one could answer them.

Both Mr. Goldworthy and Alice watched over the sufferer during that night. Towards morning, he revived sufficiently to tell them all he knew of the dreadful occurrence which had taken place. His chamber adjoined that of Fanny; he had been aroused from his slumbers by her piercing scream; instantly leaping from his bed, he rushed into the young lady's apartment, and saw a tall, black-visaged ruffian standing over her apparently insensible form, in the act of dragging her from the couch. The villain turned suddenly, drew a pistol upon the young gentleman, and fired. Clarence fell, severely wounded, and remained unconscious of everything, until he found himself stretched upon a bed of pain, with his uncle and cousin watching him with affectionate solicitude.

On learning that poor Fanny had disappeared—undoubtedly carried off by the ruffian whom he had seen in her chamber—the grief and rage of Clarence knew no bounds. Regardless of his wound and sufferings, he would have arisen from his bed and gone in pursuit of the ravisher, had he not been restrained by his more considerate relatives, who represented to him the folly and danger of his undertaking such a hopeless task, in his precarious state of health. Overcome by their united persuasions, as well as by a consciousness of his own bodily weakness, he contented himself with his uncle's assurance that every effort would immediately be made to discover the whereabouts of poor Fanny, and restore her to her friends.

Early the next morning, Corporal Grimsby, as being the friend and guardian of the missing girl, was apprised of the fact of her abduction. It is needless for us to repeat all the singular oaths with which the eccentric, good old man expressed his honest indignation, when he received the alarming intelligence; suffice it to say, he swore by the nose of Napoleon, and by his own whiskers, (an oath which he used only on very solemn occasions,) never to rest until he had discovered Fanny, his darling *protege*, and severely punished her rascally kidnapper.

A dark suspicion crossed his mind that the villain Tickels was at the bottom of the business; acting upon the first impulse of the moment, he instantly proceeded to the residence of the old libertine, forced his way into his presence, and boldly accused him of the deed. Mr. Tickels was perfectly on his guard, for he had expected such a visit; with cool politeness he assured the Corporal that until that moment he knew nothing of the matter; he was sorry that his *friend* should suspect him of any participation in such a piece of rascality; he had long since cleansed and purified himself of the wicked and silly passion which he at one time felt for Miss Aubrey; he sincerely hoped that nothing unpleasant would befall her; he'd do all in his power to seek her out; and concluded by coolly inviting the Corporal to breakfast with him.

"Breakfast with the devil!" cried the old man, indignantly—"sooner would I sit down to table in social companionship with—with *Jew Mike* himself!" and as he uttered these words, he gazed keenly into the other's countenance. Tickels started, and turned deadly pale; the Corporal, with a sarcastic smile, bowed with mock politeness, and withdrew.

"Swords and carving-knives! I thought so," he muttered, after he had left the house—"a masterly stroke, that; a masterly stroke! This villain Jew Mike is the *cher amie* of Sow Nance, as she is called; and Nance is in the confidence of Tickels; what wonder that the dirty slut recommended her *pal* and paramour to the old libertine, as a fit agent to abduct my poor Fanny—and what wonder that he was employed to accomplish that object? But first, I'll hasten to Mr. Goldworthy's house, and question the young man who was wounded; if his description of the villain corresponds with the appearance of Jew Mike, then there can be no further doubt on the subject, and I shall know what course to pursue. Egad! how old Tickels changed color when I mentioned Jew Mike! His confusion alone indicated his guilt. 'Sdeath; I have no time to lose; may heaven preserve and guard that poor, persecuted orphan girl!"

On reaching Mr. Goldworthy's house, he requested to be conducted immediately to Clarence's chamber. In answer to his inquiries, the young man stated that the villain who had wounded him was a tall, powerfully built person, his face almost entirely concealed by a profusion of black hair. The Corporal rubbed his hands with glee.

"Jew Mike, by the bones of the great Mogul!" he exclaimed—"and now that I am on the right scent, I shall soon ferret out the ravenous wolves that have carried my poor lamb to their infernal den. Ah, Corporal Grimsby, thou art a cunning dog!" So saying, he departed on his benevolent errand of endeavoring to rescue Fanny Aubrey from the power of her enemies.

That evening, from every window of Mr. Goldworthy's princely mansion in Howard street, shone brilliant lights. It was the eve appointed for the marriage of Alice and the Chevalier Duvall.

In consequence of the melancholy and startling events which took place in the house on the preceding night—the severe wounding of Clarence, and the abduction of Fanny—it had been suggested by both Alice and her father, that it would be proper to defer the performance of the ceremony for a short time, or until the fate of the missing girl could be ascertained; the Chevalier, however, strongly opposed this proposition, and assuming the authority of an accepted suitor, delicately but firmly insisted that the marriage should take place that evening, as had been previously arranged "for," said he, "to defer the consummation of our happiness will not assist in the recovery of

Miss Aubrey. When I become your husband, my Alice, I can with far more propriety aid in seeking the lost one, for were we to remain unmarried, my interest in the poor young lady might be imputed to improper or even dishonorable motives."

This reasoning had the desired effect; it was decided that the marriage ceremony should not be postponed.

Alice had not communicated to the Chevalier the story which Fanny had told her, concerning the affair of the lost package of money—for as she utterly disbelieved the tale, (imputing it to the effects of an excited imagination,) she had no desire to wound the feelings of her lover by acquainting him with the absurd charge (as she thought) which had been brought against him. How blind is love to the imperfections, the faults, and even the crimes of the object of its adoration! We believe it is Shakespeare who says:

> "Love looks not with the eye, but with the mind,
> And therefore is wing'd Cupid painted blind."

The folding doors which separated the two spacious parlors in Mr. Goldworthy's house were thrown open, forming a vast hall, brilliantly illuminated by superb chandeliers, and decorated with every appliance of modern elegance and taste. About a dozen relatives and friends of the family had assembled to witness the ceremony; among them were several of the wealthiest members of the Boston aristocracy. There was the gray-headed millionaire, who has made his name famous by the magnificence of his donations to public institutions which are already wealthy enough; but then such liberal gifts are heralded in the newspapers, and his name is blazoned forth as the great philanthropist; and—it really is so troublesome to give to the suffering poor; besides, the world seldom hears of deeds of unostentatious charity. Now, we are one of those plain people who like to look at things in the light of common reason, without regard to high-sounding titles, or lofty associations; and it is our unpretending opinion that the God of charity and mercy looks down with much greater approbation upon the act of feeding a starving family, or comfortably clothing a few of His naked little ones, than upon the bestowal of twenty or thirty thousand dollars on this or that University, for the purpose of endowing a Professor of Humbugonomy, that he may initiate a class of learned blockheads into the mysteries of star-gazing, patient-killing, legal fleecing, or cheating the devil by turning parson.

Besides the gray-headed millionaire, to whom we have thus particularly alluded, there was the young lady who boasts of being heiress to hundreds of thousands of dollars; consequently, of course, she is unanimously voted to be "charming—divine—perfection!" Her beauty is pronounced angelic; her accomplishments are the theme of universal admiration. "Oh, she is an unsurpassable creature!" exclaim the whole tribe of contemptible, sycophantic, brainless calves in broadcloth, who are ever ready to fall down and worship the golden emblem of themselves. And yet she is pug-nosed, freckle-faced, and red-headed; insolent to her equals, coarsely familiar with her inferiors; her vulgarity is without wit, her affectation is devoid of elegance or grace; ignorant and stupid, the meanest kitchen wench would suffer by a comparison with her. In striking contrast with this ludicrous specimen of degraded aristocracy, there were several young ladies present who were really lovely and accomplished women. These were the personal friends of Alice; they had come to witness her nuptials with the magnificent Chevalier.

Precisely as the clock struck eight, Duvall entered the apartment, and saluted the company with that exquisite and gentlemanly grace for which he was distinguished. With difficulty could the assembled guests refrain from expressing their admiration aloud; for his appearance was singularly grand and imposing. In his dress, not the slightest approach to foppery could be detected; all was faultless elegance. In his dark eyes and on his proud features an observer could read the lofty triumph which he felt; for was not he, an unknown and perhaps penniless adventurer, about to wed the beautiful and accomplished daughter of one of Boston's "merchant princes"?

Soon the clergyman arrived, and Alice was summoned to take her part in the solemn ceremony which was about to be performed. She was dressed in simple white, her only ornaments consisting of a few natural flowers among the rich clusters of her shining hair.

She was very beautiful; the flush of happiness suffused her cheeks—her eyes sparkled with ineffable joy. Oh, terrible sacrifice!

The ceremony proceeds; the solemn words are spoken. 'Tis all over—friends crowd around with their congratulations—there are smiles, and blushes, and tears; but a deep sense of happiness pervades every heart. Alice is the wife of Duvall, by the sacred rites of the church, in the sight of Heaven, and before men. The Chevalier pressed her madly to his heart, while

> "Unto the ground she cast her modest eye,
> And, ever and anon, with rosy red,
> The bashful blush her snowy cheeks did dye."

Then came music, and the merry dance—and finally, a repast, that rivalled in luxury the banquet of an emperor. In the midst of the supper, in obedience to the secret signal of one of her bridesmaids, Alice stole away, and was conducted by a charming *coterie* of her female friends, to Hymen's sacred retreat, the nuptial chamber—which nothing should induce us to invade, gentle reader, were it not necessary to do so in order to develop a scene in our narrative, which cannot possibly be omitted.

It was an apartment of but moderate size; yet it was a gem of luxurious comfort. Everything was in the most perfect taste; and it was evident by a certain refined delicacy in all the arrangements, that the fair Alice herself had superintended the preparations. Happy the man who should bestow the first chaste kiss of wedded love, upon the pure lips of a lovely bride, within that soft bower of voluptuousness!

She is disrobed; from her virgin limbs are removed the snowy garments; she is coquettishly arrayed in the seductive costume of bewitching night! She blushes, and is almost painfully embarrassed; for never before have her glowing charms been contemplated thus, even by female eyes. She finds herself at last reclining within the luxurious folds of the magnificent nuptial couch; then her kind friends kiss her—bid her a smiling good-night—and leave her to await the coming of her husband. For the first time, her bosom heaves tumultuously with emotions which she acknowledges to be delightful, though she cannot comprehend them.

But where, meanwhile, is the happy bridegroom? He is at the head of the splendid board, responding to the many toasts which are proposed in his honor, and that of his lovely and expectant bride. Again and again he fills the goblet, and quaffs the foaming champagne. He fascinates everybody by his rare eloquence—his inimitable wit; Mr. Goldworthy congratulates himself on his good fortune in having secured so charming—so talented a son-in-law. The dark eyes of the Chevalier sparkle almost fearfully; his superb countenance is flushed with wine and passion. This rosy god of the grape has nearly conquered him; he is more than half intoxicated. Losing his habitual caution, he launches forth into the recital of the most brilliant and daring adventures in intrigue, fraud and robbery, he relates these events with a gusto that would seem to indicate his having taken a leading part in them himself. The guests are startled, and view him with an admiration mixed with fear. The Chevalier drinks deeper and deeper. Wilder and more exciting grow his narratives; he tells strange tales of the Italian banditti—of pirates upon the Spanish main—of dashing French pickpockets—of bold English highwaymen—of desperate American burglars, and of expert counterfeiters. Mr. Goldworthy, at last, begins to regard him with a feeling akin to suspicion. "Who can this man be," he mentally asks himself—"that talks so familiarly of every species of crime and villainy? Is he a fitting husband for my pure and gentle daughter? Can he have been a participant in those lawless adventures which he so eloquently describes? I like not the dark frown upon his brow, nor the fierce glances of his eyes. But tush! of what am I thinking? I must not harbor unjust suspicions against the husband of my child; he is merely somewhat excited by the generous wine, and probably derived his knowledge of these matters from the romances of the day. 'Tis best that he should drink no more at present; I will therefore hint to him that it is high time for a loyal bridegroom to retire to the arms of his expectant bride. He surely will not disregard so tempting a suggestion, for my Alice is very like her mother, and egad! on *my* wedding night, twenty years ago, I needed no second hint to induce me to fly eagerly to *her* arms. Ah, I was young then, and old age plays sad havoc with us!"

The worthy old gentleman whispered a few moments in the ear of the Chevalier. The latter arose with a flushed cheek and a flashing eye.

"Thanks for the hint, good father-in-law," he cried, draining another goblet of wine—"I have paid my devoirs to Bacchus; now will I worship at the shrine of Venus!"

With rather an unsteady gait he left the apartment, and, under the guidance of two lovely, blushing, tittering damsels, sought the nuptial chamber. At the door of that sacred retreat, his fair guides left him. He entered—and the black-hearted villain, stained with a thousand crimes, stood in the presence of angel purity.

And now, fain would we draw a curtain over what followed—but if we did so, our task would be incomplete. We therefore pass over the delicate details with as much rapidity as the nature of the case will admit.

The Chevalier advanced to the couch, and viewed his bride; evading his ardent gaze, she turned away, her maiden cheek glowing with blushes. Upon the snowy pillow, in rich masses, lay her luxuriant hair; her modestly veiled bosom, whose voluptuousness of outline no drapery could entirely conceal, heaved tumultuously with gushing joy, and holy happiness, and pure passion, and maidenly fear. Her small, exquisite hand, on whose taper fore-finger glittered a magnificent diamond ring, (her husband's gift,) rested upon the gorgeous counterpane, like a snow-flake upon a cluster of roses.

Still the Chevalier profanes not that pure form with his unhallowed touch; perchance some unseen power, the guardian of spotless innocence, restrains him. Placing himself before the splendid mirror, he begins to remove his superb garments with a deliberation and a composure that astonishes even himself.

As each article of dress is successively thrown aside, the magnificent symmetry of that man's unrivalled form becomes more and more apparent. Though of a build unusually powerful, his limbs possess all the grace and suppleness of the Apollo Belvedere. He is one of those rare combinations of strength and beauty, so often represented by classic statuary, yet so seldom seen in a living model.

His task is at length completed; he is in the primeval costume of nature. Complacently he surveys his reflection in the mirror; for he is fully conscious of his great personal advantages, and, in the vanity of his heart, he wishes to display them to the enraptured gaze of his bride. And she—who will say that she does not stealthily contemplate his symmetrical proportions with secret satisfaction—for what woman could, under such peculiar circumstances, be indifferent to the physical advantages possessed by the man of her choice?

Alas! how suddenly did poor Alice's golden dream of happiness vanish forever!

For there—upon her husband's naked breast—in black characters of damning distinctness—is *branded* the ghastly, hideous words—"CONVICTED FELON!!"

Alice uttered one piercing scream, and fainted.

The marriage guests below had not yet departed. They heard that awful cry, which seemed to be the very concentration of all human anguish. Mr. Goldworthy started to his feet, and his cheeks grew ashy pale.

"My friends," said he, in a low tone—"there is something wrong with my child. Remain here, and I will ascertain the cause of this strange outcry."

Having armed himself with a pistol, he repaired to his daughter's chamber, which he entered without ceremony; for when does a father stand on ceremony, when he believes the safety of his only child to be in danger? There, in the centre of the room, confused and abashed, stood the nude form of the Chevalier; and there, upon his breast, did Mr. Goldworthy behold the accursed brand of crime which had horrified his daughter, and elicited her piercing scream.

"*Convicted felon!*" gasped the old gentleman, almost disbelieving the evidence of his own senses. "Good God! am I dreaming, or do I actually behold that awful badge of infamy branded upon the flesh of the husband of my child! Almighty heaven, thy judgments are inscrutable, but this blow is too much—too much!"

He buried his face in his hands, and wept bitterly. The Chevalier, by a powerful effort, recovered his accustomed assurance and presence of mind.

"Come, my good sir," said he—"don't get in such a bad way about a few insignificant letters which are stamped upon me. I pledge you my honor 'twas merely done in jest, in a thoughtless moment. Pray retire, and leave me to console my bride for her silly fright."

"Liar and villain!" cried the old man—"would'st thou, with a red-hot iron, brand such words as *those* upon thee, in jest? Thou are a convicted scoundrel—an impostor—a murderer, for aught I know. Thou hast no claim upon my poor girl, who now lies there, insensible; the marriage is null and void!"

"Pooh—nonsense!" said the Chevalier, very coolly—"you make a devil of a fuss about a very small matter. This brand is but the consequence of a youthful folly—crime, if you will—of which I have long since repented, I assure you. A ruffled shirt will always conceal it from the world's prying gaze; your daughter and yourself are the only persons who will ever know of its existence; why, then, should it interfere with our matrimonial arrangements?"

"Dare you parley with me, villain?" cried Mr. Goldworthy, growing more and more indignant at the other's impudent assurance. "Hark'ee, sir," he continued, "the mystery which has always surrounded you, has been anything but favorable to your reputation, for *honest* men are seldom reluctant to disclose all that concerns their past career and present pursuits. But your damnable effrontery, and the accursed fascination of your manners, overcame all our suspicions relative to you; you were regarded as an honorable man, and a gentleman. Unfortunately, my Alice loved you, and in an evil moment I consented to your union. This evening, at the wine table, when you discoursed so learnedly and eloquently upon the exploits of daring villains, the thought struck me that you must have derived your knowledge of them from personal intimacy; but I instantly discarded the suspicion as unworthy of myself and unjust to you. But now—now your guilt can no longer be questioned, for its history is written there, upon your breast! Scoundrel, I might hand you over to the iron grasp of the law, but I will not; resume your garments, and leave this chamber—for your vile presence contaminates the very atmosphere, and 'tis no place for you!"

"No, you will not hand me over to the law, neither will you expose me," said the Chevalier, his lip curling with proud disdain. "Listen to me, old man: you are right—I *am* a villain—nay, more; I glory in the title. Am I not candid with you?—and yet you, yourself, will be as anxious as I can be, to keep the world ignorant of the fact that I am a villain,—for will the aristocratic Mr. Goldworthy consent that the public shall know that his beautiful daughter Alice is married to a branded criminal? Being perfectly safe, what need is there of concealment on my part? Know, then, that I am an escaped convict from Botany Bay, to which colony I was transported from England, for an atrocious crime. This brand upon my breast was placed there as a punishment for having attempted to murder one of my guards. I have been a pirate, a robber, a highwayman, a burglar, and (but let me whisper this word in your ear,) a *murderer*! Ha, ha, ha! how do you like your son-in-law now?"

"Monster, out of my sight!" cried the old man, shuddering.

"Softly, softly," said the Chevalier, with imperturbable calmness—"you have not heard all yet; of my skill as a pickpocket, you yourself have had ample proof, for 'twas I who relieved you of the valuable package last night; yet you dare not prosecute me—for am I not your son-in-law? But curses on my own indiscretion, in allowing wine to overcome my habitual prudence! For had I not been partially intoxicated, think you this mark of guilt would have been so easily discovered? No, believe me—"

"Silence, villain!" thundered Mr. Goldworthy, no longer able to contain his indignation at the cool effrontery of the Chevalier—"I have bandied words with you too long already; you see this pistol?—you are unarmed; I give you five minutes to dress yourself and leave the house; if you are not gone at the end of that time, I swear by the living God to shoot you through the head."

These last words were pronounced with a calmness that left no doubt of their sincerity on the mind of the Chevalier. Villain as he was, he was brave even to desperation; yet he had no particular wish to be hurried into eternity so unceremoniously. He therefore commenced dressing himself, while Mr. Goldworthy stood with the pistol cocked and pointed at his head with a deadly aim.

Meanwhile, the unfortunate Alice recovered from her swoon. Starting up in bed, she cast a hurried glance at her father and the discomfited Chevalier. That glance was sufficient to reveal to her the true state of affairs; and covering her face with her hands, she wept bitterly.

Who can comprehend the depth and devotedness of woman's love? Could it be possible that there still lingered in her crushed heart a single atom of affection for that branded villain, who had so cruelly deceived her? Philosophy may condemn her—human reason itself may scoff at her—but from her pure heart could not utterly be obliterated the sincere and holy love which she had conceived for that unworthy object. To her might have been applied the beautiful words of the poet Campbell:

"Let the eagle change his plume,
The leaf its hue, the flower its bloom,
But ties around that heart were spun
Which would not, could not be undone."

Before the expiration of the prescribed five minutes, the Chevalier was dressed, and ready to depart. Turning towards Alice, he regarded her with a look which was eloquently expressive of grief, remorse and sorrow. His breast heaved convulsively; he was evidently struggling with the most powerful emotions. A single tear rolled down his cheek—he hastily wiped it away—murmured, "Farewell, Alice, forever!"—and reminded by an imperious gesture from her father that the scene could continue no longer, he turned calmly and walked out of the room. Mr. Goldworthy followed him to the street door, and saw him depart from the house; then, with a deep-drawn sigh, he returned to his guests, who were naturally eager to know the nature of the difficulty. In answer to their inquiries, the old gentleman said—

"My dear friends, do not, I entreat you, press me for an explanation of this most melancholy affair. Suffice it for me to say, the Chevalier Duvall has proved himself to be utterly unworthy of my daughter. The marriage which has taken place, though not legally void, is *morally* so. I beg of everyone present to respect my feelings as a father and as a man, so far as to preserve a strict silence in reference to this painful matter. The Chevalier Duvall has departed from the house, and will never see my daughter more."

The required promise was given, and the guests took their leave, experiencing feelings of a far different nature from those which had animated them at the commencement of the evening. They had come in the happy anticipation of witnessing the consummation of a beloved friend's felicity; they went away oppressed by a painful uncertainty as to the nature of the difficulty which had arisen in reference to the husband, and chilled by a fear that the earthly happiness of poor Alice was destroyed forever.

The Chevalier returned to the Duchess, to apprise her of the total ruin of his matrimonial schemes, in consequence of the *fatal brand* upon his person having been discovered; and we return to Fanny Aubrey, who had been conveyed by Jew Mike to the *"Chambers of Love,"* in obedience to the directions given him by the Hon. Timothy Tickels.

Chapter VII
Showing the operations of Jew Mike and his coadjutors.—The necessity of young ladies looking beneath their beds, before retiring to rest

We have seen in what manner Jew Mike escaped from the house of Mr. Goldworthy, bearing off the insensible form of Fanny Aubrey; but as the reader may be curious to learn how the ruffian gained entrance to the house, and to the chamber of the young lady, we shall briefly explain.

In the first place, it is perhaps understood that old Tickels applied to Sow Nance for assistance in the business of abducting Fanny, and conveying her to that den of iniquity called the "Chambers of Love,"—which place will be hereafter described. Nance, on being applied to, informed her employer that she had a *"love cull,"* (paramour,) who was exactly suited to the business, and who would, for a proper compensation, engage to do the job. Tickels was delighted with the proposal, and eagerly desired to have an early interview with her accommodating lover. But there was a difficulty; Jew Mike had an invincible repugnance to going abroad under any circumstances, inasmuch as he had recently been engaged in a heavy burglary, and the pleasure of his company was earnestly sought after by police officer Storkfeather and other indefatigables. He was safely housed in the "Pig Pen," and regarded it as decidedly unsafe to venture out, even to execute a piece of work as profitable as the one which Mr. Tickels wished him to perform. It was finally arranged that the latter gentleman would call on Mike at the "Pen," on a certain evening. This was done; and the result of that interview was, that Mike, for and in consideration of receiving the sum of one hundred dollars, agreed to carry off Fanny Aubrey, and deposit her safely in the "Chambers of Love."

To obviate the possibility of Mike's being overhauled by his old friends the police officers, it was arranged that a cab should be at his entire disposal; the same vehicle would serve to convey the young lady with secrecy and rapidity to the place destined for her imprisonment. Tickels engaged to have Mike privately introduced into the house of Mr. Goldworthy, and it was effected in this manner.

On the night previous to the abduction, at about the hour of nine, a cab was driven through Ann street, and halted in front of the dance cellar which communicated with the "Pig Pen." The driver of this vehicle was a sable individual, who has since attained some notoriety under the cognomen of "Jonas." He is intimately acquainted with the location and condition of every house of prostitution in Boston, and enjoys the familiar acquaintance of many white courtezans of beauty and fashion, not a few of whom (so 'tis said,) testify their appreciation of his valuable services in bringing them profitable custom, by freely granting him those delightful privileges which are usually extended to white patrons only, who can pay well for the same. Jonas has lately become the editor and proprietor of that valuable periodical known as the "Key to the Chambers of Love," which is a *card* containing a list of almost every bower of pleasure in Boston, with the names of their keepers. It is a document which is extensively patronized by the sporting bloods. This fortunate darkey it was, then, who was employed in the delicate matter, the progress of which we are now describing.

He had no sooner halted his cab, as we have stated, than there cautiously issued from the cellar an individual carefully concealed from observation by a huge slouched hat and cloak. This, it is almost needless to say, was Jew Mike himself. Having greeted Jonas with the assurance of "all right," he quickly entered the cab, and the sable driver started his horse towards Howard street at a slapping pace.

In the neighborhood of the Athenaeum, the cab paused, and Mike got out. He was instantly joined by the Hon. Mr. Tickels, who said to Jonas—

"Drive away, and be on this spot again, with your horse and cab, precisely at twelve o'clock. Remain here until one; if by that time Mike does not make his appearance, you will know that the job can't be done to-night, and you need wait no longer. To-morrow night, be on this spot again, at twelve, and remain until one—and don't fail to repeat this every night until Mike appears with the young woman he is to carry off. For every night that you come here, you shall be paid five dollars. Do you understand?"

"Yes, indeed, ole hoss," replied the delighted Jonas, displaying his mouthful of dominoes—"dat five dollars ebery night will 'nable dis colored person to shine at de balls of de colored society dis winter; perhaps be de manager—yah, yah, yah!" When giving utterance to his peculiar laugh, Jonas makes a noise as if he were undergoing the process of being choked to death by a fat sausage. Having thus given vent to his satisfaction, he mounted his cab and drove off. When he had departed, Tickels drew Mike within the dark shadow of a building, and, in whispered tones, thus addressed him:—

"I have, as you are aware, succeeded in bribing one of Goldworthy's servants to admit you into the house, and conceal you until the favorable moment arrives for you to bear off the prize. Whether you do it to-night, or to-morrow night, or the next, you must be sure to do it only between the hours of twelve and one, for only during that interval of time will Jonas and his cab be in waiting for you. When the time for action arrives, you must satisfy yourself that all is still in the house—that all have retired. I have ascertained that Goldworthy and his household almost invariably retire to rest at ten o'clock; therefore, it is reasonable to suppose that they are all asleep by twelve. At that hour, if you think the coast is clear, steal cautiously forth from your place of concealment, and noiselessly enter the young lady's chamber; this you will have no difficulty in doing, for I have taken the pains to ascertain that she never takes the precaution to lock the door."

"But," interrupted Jew Mike—"in that large mansion, containing so many apartments, how shall I know for certainty which particular room the young woman sleeps in?"

"I have anticipated and provided for that difficulty," rejoined Tickels—"although the servant whom I have bribed, could doubtless direct you to the chamber. Here, on this sheet of paper, I have drawn a diagram of the entire building; by studying it for a few minutes, you will readily be enabled to find your way to any part of the house.—To resume: you will enter the chamber, and assure yourself that the young lady is sleeping; this is an important point, because, if she should chance to be awake, and observe you, she would naturally scream with affright, which would ruin everything. Well, having satisfied yourself, beyond a doubt, that she is fast asleep, you will softly approach the bed, and, in the twinkling of an eye, *bind and gag her!* so that she will be utterly incapable of voice or motion. Then take her in your arms, steal noiselessly down stairs, and make your exit by the front door, which will be left unlocked for that purpose. Having reached the street, leap with your precious burden into the cab, and Jonas will drive you with all speed to the 'Chambers.' Take off your shoes when in the house, and your footsteps will be less liable to be heard. Now, Mike, I have one request to make: I know the laxity of your principles with respect to the virtue of honesty, and admire your system of appropriation—but steal nothing, not even the merest trifle, in the house. I will tell you why I require this of you; when the young lady is missed, if property is also missed, they will naturally suppose that both she and the valuables have been carried off by some marauder; for they could never believe *her* to be guilty of theft; and their affection for her would prompt them to make every effort for her recovery. If, on the contrary, no property disappears with her, they may possibly think that she has voluntarily eloped, and will be apt to trouble themselves very little about her, for her supposed ingratitude will arouse their indignation. Do you not perceive and acknowledge the force of my argument?"

Jew Mike replied that he certainly did, and assured his worthy employer that he would, for the first time in his life, refrain from stealing, even where he had an excellent opportunity.

"This heroic self-denial on your part is worthy of the highest commendation," said Mr. Tickels. "I have but one more observation to make, and then I will detain you no longer. If it should unfortunately happen that you are detected in this business, for God's sake don't bring my name in connection with it. Tell them that your design was to rob the house; they will send you to jail, and no matter how many charges may be brought against you, I have money and influence sufficient to procure your liberation. Now, my good fellow, do you consent to this?"

Mike answered affirmatively; and the two proceeded towards Mr. Goldworthy's house. Fortunately for their operations, there was no moon, and the night was intensely dark; therefore, they were by no means likely to be observed by any prying individual or inquisitive Charley—besides, the gentlemen who belong to the latter class, prefer rather to indulge in a comfortable doze on some door-step, than to go prowling about, impertinently interfering with the business of enterprising burglars and others, who "prefer darkness rather than light."

The Hon. Mr. Tickels and Jew Mike, having reached Mr. Goldworthy's house, stationed themselves in front of the door, and after a short pause, to assure themselves that all was right, the former worthy gave utterance to three distinct coughs, which were, however, rendered in a very low tone. The signal was answered almost immediately; the door was softly opened, and a man made his appearance; this was the unfaithful servant who had been bribed to admit a villain into his master's house.

"Is everything all right, Cushing?" asked Tickels, in a whisper.

"Yes, sir," replied the fellow, in the same tone—"there's no one stirring in the house except myself, as Mr. Goldworthy and the ladies have gone to the theatre, and have not yet returned; and as to the other servants, they have all gone to bed."

"That's well," remarked Tickels—"now, Mike, this man will conceal you in some safe place. If the business can be done to-night, do it; if not, defer it until a favorable opportunity presents itself. You know all the arrangements; therefore I need not repeat them. Fulfil your contract, and come to me for your reward. Good night."

He departed. Cushing desired Jew Mike to follow him into the house; the latter obeyed, and was conducted into a small room, which the servant gave him to understand was his sleeping chamber.

"Is this to be my place of concealment?" demanded Jew Mike, glancing around with a growl of dissatisfaction—"damn it, you couldn't hide a mouse here without its being discovered."

"That's true enough," rejoined Cushing—"you can't hide here, that's certain. I confess I am at a loss where to put you. There's no time to be lost, for I expect my master and the ladies to return every instant. Hell and furies, there's the carriage now! they have come!"

It was true; a carriage stopped at the door, and they could hear the voices and footsteps of people entering the house.

"We are lost!" cried Cushing, pale with fear—"yet stay; there is but one way of escaping immediate detection. Have you the courage to hide in—in—"

"Courage!" exclaimed Mike, in great rage—"show me a place of concealment, and I'll stow myself in it, if it be hell itself! Our enterprise must not fail by my being discovered here."

"Quick, then—this way—follow me—softly, softly," whispered the other, conducting Mike up a flight of stairs, and into a handsomely furnished bed-chamber.

"This," said Cushing—"is the room in which Miss Fanny Aubrey sleeps; the young lady whom you are to carry off. It is the best place in the world for you to conceal yourself in, for your victim will be almost within your grasp. Quick—stow yourself *under the bed,* in the farthest corner. She will not discover you, if you keep perfectly quiet, for you will be screened from view by the thick curtains of the bed. If you cannot do the job to-night, you must remain in your hiding-place all day to-morrow—and indeed, you must not think of stirring forth, until the moment arrives for you to carry off Miss Fanny. I will contrive to supply you with food and drink. Hark!—by God, somebody is coming up-stairs. I must be off—under the bed with you—quick, quick!"

In a twinkling was Jew Mike snugly ensconced beneath the bed, while Cushing hastily left the chamber, and repaired to his own room.

Within the space of one minute afterwards, Fanny Aubrey entered her chamber, accompanied by a maid-servant bearing a light.

"You may set down the candle, Matilda, if you please, dear," said Fanny, in her sweet, gentle voice—"and leave me, for I shall not need your assistance to undress me."

"Indeed, Miss, axing your pardon, I shall do no such thing," responded Matilda, who was a buxom, good-humored, and rather good-looking young woman; and with a kind of respectful familiarity, she began to perform upon her young mistress the delicate and graceful duties of a *femme de chambre*. "You are very silly, Matilda, thus to insist on waiting on *me*; I, that am as poor as yourself, and was brought up as nothing but a fruit girl."

"Lor, Miss!" cried Matilda, holding up her hands with a sort of pious horror—"how can you compare yourself with the likes of me? You were born to be a lady, and I am so happy to be your servant—your own ladies' maid! You will have a fine husband one of these days, Miss. Now, if I might make so bold, there is that pretty young gentleman, Miss Alice's cousin, Master Clarence—"

"Hush, Matilda," interrupted Fanny, blushing deeply—"what has Master Clarence to do with me? you are a silly creature. Make haste and undress me, since you will do it, for I am so tired and sleepy!"

Matilda did as she was desired, but being, like all other ladies' maids, very talkative, kept up a 'running commentary' on the charms of her young mistress, as ladies' maids are very apt to do.

"What beautiful hair!" quoth the abigail, in an under tone, as if she were merely holding a sociable chat with herself—"for all the world like skeins of golden thread; and what a fair skin! just like a heap of snow, or a newly washed sheet spread out to bleach. Patience alive! this pretty arm beats Mrs. Swelby's wax-work all hollow; and these beautiful—"

"You vex me to death with your nonsense, Matilda," cried Fanny—"how tiresome you are! Pray be silent."

Thus rebuked, the ladies' maid continued her task in silence. When the young lady was disrobed, and about to retire to bed, she was startled by a sudden exclamation of Matilda's—

"Bless me, Miss! what noise was that? It sounded as if somebody was hid somewhere in this very chamber."

They both paused and listened; all was again still. Fanny, as well as her maid had certainly heard a slight noise, which seemed to have been produced by a slow and cautious movement, and sounded like the rustling of a curtain.

"Twas nothing but the noise of the night-breeze agitating the window curtains," remarked Fanny, at length, with a smile.

Ah! neither she, nor her maid, saw the two fearful eyes that were glaring at them from among the intricate folds of the curtain, beneath the bed!— Neither saw they the dark and hideous countenance of the ruffian that lay concealed there.

"Well, Miss," said Matilda, not over half re-assured by the words of her mistress—"it may be nothing, as you say; but, for my part, I never go to bed a single night in the year, without first *looking under the bed* to see that nobody is hid away there. And I advise you to do the same, Miss; and I am sure you would, if you only knew what happened to my cousin Bridget."

"And what was that, pray?" asked Fanny, as she got into bed, and settled herself comfortably, in order to listen to what happened to cousin Bridget—all her fears in regard to the noise which she had heard, having vanished.

"Why, you see, miss," said Matilda, seating herself at the bed-side,— "cousin Bridget was cook in a gentleman's family in this city, and a very nice body she was, and is to this day. In the same family there lived a young man as was a coachman, very good-looking, and very attentive to Biddy, as we call her for shortness, miss. But, though he was desperate in love with my cousin, she would give him no encouragement, and the poor fellow pined away, and neglected his wittles, and grew thin in flesh, until, from being called Fat Tom, he got to be nicknamed the 'Natomy, which means a skeleton. It was in vain, miss, that poor 'Natomy threatened to take to hard drinking, or pizen himself with Prooshy acid, unless she took pity on him—not a smile, or a kiss, or a hope could he get from cousin Biddy. Now, between ourselves, I really think she had a sort of a sneaking notion after him; you know, miss, that we women folks like to tease the men, by making them think that we hate 'em, when all the time we are dead in love with 'em. Well, matters and things went on pretty much as I have said, for some times; until something happened that made a great change in the feelings of cousin Biddy towards Tom the coachman. Biddy slept in a nice little bed-room in the attic—all by herself; and Tom slept in another nice little bed-room in the attic—all by *himself*, too. Well, miss, one night Biddy went to a fancy ball in Ann street, given in honor of her brother's wife's second cousin, Mrs. MacFiggins, having been blessed with three twins at a birth; she danced very late, and drank a great deal of hot toddy, which made her so nervous that she had to go home in a hackney-coach. She went to bed, but the toddy made her feel so very uncomfortable, that she had to get up again, during the night; and she happened, by accident, to reach her hand under the bed—and what do you think, miss? her hand caught hold of something—she pulled it towards her, out from under the bed—and oh, my gracious! what must have been the feelings of the poor body, when she found that she had taken hold of a man's—*nose!* and, what was worse than all, that nose belonged to Tom, the coachman! My poor cousin Biddy, on making this awful discovery, gave a low scream, and fainted; and then—and then, miss—in about half an hour, when she came to her senses, on finding that nobody, except Tom, had heard her scream, she felt so kind of *put out* about the whole matter, that she agreed to marry Tom, if he would promise never to say nothing about it. He agreed, and in a few weeks afterwards they were man and wife. I heard this story, miss, from Biddy's own lips, and it's as true as gospel. So that is the reason why I look under my bed every night, to see if anybody is hid away there; because the very idea of having a man *under* a body's bed, is so awful! But bless me, miss—you are fast asleep already, and I dare say you haven't heard half of my story."

 Matilda was right; Fanny had fallen asleep at the most interesting point of the foregoing narrative, and she was therefore in blissful ignorance of the catastrophe by which cousin Biddy became the wife of Tom the coachman. The ladies' maid, muttering her indignation at the very little interest manifested in her story, by her young mistress, left the chamber, and took herself off to bed, leaving the candle burning upon the table.

 Half an hour passed; all throughout the house was profoundly still. The deep and regular breathing of Fanny indicated that she slept soundly. A small clock in the chamber proclaimed the hour of midnight. Scarce had the tiny sounds died away in silence, when the hideous head of Jew Mike cautiously emerged from beneath the bed. The ruffian noiselessly crept forth from his place of concealment, and stood over the fair sleeper. Having satisfied himself of the soundness of her slumbers, he drew from his pocket the handkerchief and cord with which he intended to gag and bind her.

At that moment, Fanny stirred, and partially awoke; quick as lightning, Jew Mike crouched down upon the carpet, and crawled beneath the bed. To his inexpressible mortification and rage, the young lady arose from the couch, advanced to the table, and having snuffed the candle, and thrown a shawl over her shoulders, seated herself, and taking up a book, began to read. The truth is, she felt herself rather restless and unwell, and determined to while away an hour or so by perusing a few chapters in the work of a favorite author.

The clock struck one, and then Jew Mike knew that his villainous plans could not be carried out that night. A few minutes afterwards, the negro Jones, who had, since twelve o'clock, been waiting with his horse and cab near Mr. Goldworthy's house in Howard street, drove off—the sable genius muttering, as he urged his 'fast crab' onward—

"Five dollars for to-night, and five dollars more for to-morrow night—dat I'm sure of, any how; gorry, dis nigger's in luck."

After the lapse of fifteen or twenty minutes, Fanny Aubrey closed her book, and again retired to bed. Again she slept; and for that night, she was safe. Mike knew that the cab had departed, and was obliged to defer the execution of his scheme until the next night, or even for a longer period, if a favorable opportunity did not then occur.

Poor Fanny! during the remainder of that night her slumbers were attended by peaceful and pleasant dreams. What if she had known that beneath her couch there lurked a desperate and bloody ruffian, impatiently awaiting the hour when he could bear her off to a fate worse than death!

Slowly wore the night away; and at length the cheerful rays of the morning sun, shining upon the beautiful countenance of the fair sleeper, awoke her from her slumbers. She arose—gracefully as a young fawn did she spring from the chaste embraces of her luxurious couch, and caroling forth a gay air—the gushing gladness of her happy heart—she proceeded to perform the duties of her toilet. Now, like a naiad at a fountain, does she lave that charming face and those ductile limbs in the limpid and rose-scented waters of a portable bath, sculptured in marble and supported by four little Cupids with gilded wings; then, like the fabled mermaid, does she arrange her shining hair in that style of beautiful simplicity which is so becoming, and so seldom successfully accomplished, even by women of undoubted taste. The amorous mirror glowingly reflects her young and budding charms, as she coquettishly admires the loveliness of her delicious little person, half-blushing at the sight of her own voluptuous nudity. Little does she suspect that the savage eyes of a concealed ruffian are gloating with lecherous delight upon her exposed form!

In happy unconsciousness of this hideous scrutiny, the young lady having completed the preliminary arrangements of her toilet, proceeded to array herself in a charming and delicate morning costume. Although it could not be said that

> "Her snowy breast was bare to ready spoil
> Of hungry eyes,"

yet these lines from *Thomson's Seasons* might be applied to her, with peculiar force:—

> "Her polished limbs
> Veil'd in a simple robe, their best attire,
> Beyond the pomp of dress; for loveliness
> Needs not the foreign aid of ornament,
> But is, when unadorn'd, adorn'd the most."

She was scarcely dressed, when the breakfast bell sounded its welcome peal; and she hastened below to take her place at the hospitable family table.

During the whole of that day, Jew Mike did not venture to stir once from his retreat. In the forenoon, a female domestic came and arranged the bed, without discovering him; after a while, Fanny came into the chamber, to dress for dinner, which being done, she withdrew without suspecting the presence of the villainous Jew Mike, who again had an opportunity of feasting his eyes on her denuded charms. Late in the afternoon, much to the joy of the ruffian, who was half starved, Cushing stole into the chamber, bringing with him some provisions and a bottle of wine; those he hastily passed under the bed, and abruptly retired, for he was apprehensive of being detected in the room, which would have ruined all.

Night came on. Mike was a witness of the scene which took place between Alice Goldworthy and Fanny, wherein the latter charged the Chevalier with having stolen the packet of money. The reader knows how Fanny was afterwards awakened from her sleep by a horrid dream, and how she discovered the form of a man bending over her—that man was, of course, Jew Mike. It will be recollected that the young girl screamed and fainted; that Clarence Argyle rushed into the chamber, and was instantly shot down by Mike—and that the ruffian made his escape from the house, bearing off the unfortunate girl in his arms.

Jonas was waiting at a short distance from the house; Mike hastily entered the cab with his burden, and the negro drove rapidly towards Warren street, wherein was located the "Chambers of Love."

The vehicle halted before a house of decent exterior; Jew Mike came out, bearing the still insensible girl; the door of the house opened, and he entered; then the door closed, and all was still. With a low chuckle of satisfaction, Jonas whipped his horse into a gallop, and away he rattled through the silent and deserted streets.

Chapter VIII
The Chambers of Love.—Conclusion

On entering the house in Warren street with his burden, Jew Mike passed through a dark passage, and entered a large, well-lighted and well-furnished room. Here he was received by a rather stout and extremely good-looking female, the landlady of the house, who rejoiced in the peculiar title of Madame Hearthstone. Notwithstanding the lateness of the hour, several courtezans of the ordinary class were lounging about, or indolently conversing with a few intimate male friends, who were probably their private lovers, or *pimps*.

"Well," said Madame Hearthstone, with a smile of satisfaction—"you have caught the bird at last, I see; but she must not remain here, for when she recovers from her swoon, she may take it into her head to scream, or make a disturbance, which might be heard in the street. We will carry her below to the *Chambers*, and there she may make as much noise as she pleases—there's no possibility of her ever being overheard by people above ground!"

In obedience to her directions, Jew Mike again took the young girl in his arms, and followed Madame out of the room, while she bore a light. She led the way into a bed-chamber on the second floor, which apartment was furnished with that luxury so invariably found in the bowers of land-ladies of pleasure, who care but little for the comfort of their *boarders*, so long as they themselves are "in clover."'

The walls of Madame's chamber were beautifully adorned with fancy paper, representing panels in gilded frames, decorated with wreaths of flowers. The lady advanced towards one of these panels, and kneeling down upon the floor, touched a secret spring; instantly a door, which had previously been invisible, sprang open, revealing an aperture large enough to admit a person standing upright.

The reader must not be surprised that the landlady should thus expose to Jew Mike the means of entering her private rendezvous; for Mike was perfectly in her confidence, having often before been employed to convey victims to that den, and being already well acquainted with the mystery of the secret panel.

They entered the aperture—the landlady bearing the light, and the ruffian carrying the unconscious form of Fanny Aubrey. Having carefully closed the panel behind them, they began to descend a long flight of steps, so steep and narrow, that extreme care was necessary to enable them to preserve their footing.

Down, down they went, seemingly far into the bowels of the earth. At length they arrived at the bottom, and a stout oaken door intercepted their further progress. The landlady produced a key, and the door swung back upon its massive hinges; they entered a vast apartment, fitted up in a style of splendor almost equal to the fabled magnificence of a fairy palace.

The hall was of circular shape, surmounted by a dome, from which hung a superb chandelier, which shed a brilliant light over the gilded ornaments and voluptuous paintings that adorned the walls. In the centre stood a table, laden with fruits and wines, around which were seated half a dozen young females, all very beautiful, and several of them nearly half naked. Two of these girls, who were more modestly dressed than the others, seemed sad and dispirited; their four companions, however, appeared vicious and reckless in the extreme.

"Girls," said the landlady, addressing them—"I have brought you a new sister; she has come to learn the delightful mysteries of Venus. Give her all the instruction in your power, and learn her the arts and ways of a finished courtezan."

Jew Mike laid Fanny upon a sofa; the girls crowded around her, and regarded her with looks of interest and joy.

"She is very pretty," said one of them, a bold, wanton looking young creature, of rare beauty, her seductive form wholly revealed beneath a single light gauze garment, such as are worn by ballet girls—"I will become her teacher; I will show her how to turn the brains of men crazy with passion, and bring the proudest of them grovelling at her feet. Oh,'tis delightful to humble the lords of creation, as they call themselves, and make them whine for our favors like so many sick spaniels!"

"You are a girl of spirit, Julia," said the landlady, regarding her with a look of admiration—"and will make a splendid courtezan."

"But," cried Julia, with sparkling eyes and a heaving breast—"when *shall* I become a courtezan? How long must I remain here, pining for the embraces of fifty men, and enduring the impotent caresses of but one, and *he*, bah! a fellow of no more fire or animation, of *power*, than a lump of ice!"

"Have patience, my love," rejoined the landlady—"Mr. Lawyer may be a poor lover, but he is a profitable patron; so long as he pays liberally for your exclusive favors in these 'Chambers,' you must receive him, for you will share the profits, when you 'turn out.' And now see what you can do in the way of restoring this new comer, for her *owner* will be here soon, to see her. Carry her into the *Satin Chamber*, which is to be her room, and when she revives, make her partake of some refreshments."

The landlady and Jew Mike left the hall; the massive door was relocked, and ascended to the upper regions of the house, leaving Fanny Aubrey to the care of the inmates of the luxurious Chambers below.

The Satin Chamber was an apartment of moderate dimensions, which adjoined the principal hall. It was completely lined throughout with white satin, which produced an effect so voluptuous as to defy description. Into this gorgeous bower of lust the girls carried Fanny, and laid her down upon a soft and yielding couch.

Restoratives were applied, and she was speedily brought to a state of consciousness. Her wonder and astonishment may easily be imagined, when, on starting up, she found herself in that strange place, surrounded by a group of showily dressed females, some of them indecently nude.

Without answering her eager inquiries, as to where she was, and how she came there, they brought her wine and other refreshments, of which they compelled her to partake.

"You are in a place of safety, and among friends," said one of them, a beautiful brunette of sixteen, whose glossy hair fell in rich masses upon her naked shoulders and bosom.—This abandoned young creature was a Jewess, named Rachel; her own wild, lascivious passions had been the cause of her being brought to the 'Chambers,' rather than the arts of the man who was at that time enjoying her delectable favors.

"Yes, dear," chimed in the voluptuous Julia—"we are your sisters, and it will be our task to teach you the delights of love, while you remain among us.—But come, girls; let us leave our sister to repose; she is a little Venus, and will dream of Cupid's pleasures, and when she awakes from her soft slumbers, she may find herself in the arms of an impetuous lover.—Happy girl! I envy her the bliss which she is soon to experience, because it is to her, as yet, a bliss *untasted*."

Each of the embryo Cyprians kissed the intended victim; some did it almost passionately, as if their libidinous natures derived a gratification even in kissing one of their own sex; some did it laughingly, with whispered words of encouragement and congratulation; but one of them, less hardened than the rest, dropped a tear of pity on her cheek, and in a gentle, yet faltering voice, murmured—"Poor girl, I am sorry for you!" They departed, and Fanny was left alone—alone with her tears, her troubled thoughts, and a thousand fears; for she remembered having seen the ruffian at her bed-side, and although she recollected nothing of what had subsequently occurred, still she doubted not that she had been carried to the place where she found herself, for some terrible purpose.

The six 'daughters of Venus' returned to the principal hall, and had scarcely resumed their places at the table, when the door was opened, and an old gentleman entered. He was a very tall, erect, slim personage, dressed in blue broadcloth, his neck neatly enveloped in a white cravat, garnished with a shirt collar of uncommon magnitude. Judging from appearances, he might formerly have been an individual of rather comely presence; but, strange to say, he was almost entirely destitute of a *nose*—the place formerly occupied by that important feature, being now supplied by a stump of flesh little larger than an ordinary pimple. This deformity gave his face an aspect extremely ludicrous, if not positively disgusting; and was the result of an indiscreet amour in former times, which not only communicated the fiery brand of destruction to his nasal organ, but also effectually disqualified him from any further direct indulgence in the amorous gambols of Venus. Thus painfully afflicted, 'Tom Lawyer,' as he has always been familiarly called, was obliged to content himself with such enjoyments as lay within the limited range of his physical powers—enjoyments which, though rather unsatisfactory, were nevertheless expensive; yet his immense wealth enabled him to command them. To explain: he would maintain in luxury some beautiful young female, with whom he would pass a portion of his leisure time in harmless dalliance—therefore was he the *patron* of the voluptuous Julia, whom he kept strictly secluded in the 'Chambers,' fearing that her unsatisfied passions would seek their 'legitimate gratification,' were an opportunity afforded her to do so.

As he entered, Julia affected the utmost delight at seeing him, and rushing into his arms, almost devoured him with kisses; and then she followed him into an adjoining chamber, her beautiful countenance wearing an expression of ill-concealed disgust.—They entered—the door was closed, and—we dare not describe what followed.

At an early hour, on the morning succeeding these events, Jew Mike called on the Hon. Mr. Tickels, for the purpose of receiving the one hundred dollars, which had been promised him as the reward of his villainy in abducting Fanny Aubrey.

On learning that the infamous project had been crowned with complete success, the old libertine was overjoyed beyond measure; but when Mike demanded the one hundred dollars, his face lengthened—for he was avaricious as well as villainous, and his recent loss of five thousand dollars, in favor of the Chevalier and the Duchess, made him exceedingly loth to part with a cool hundred so easily.—Not exactly knowing the sort of a man he had to deal with, he assumed a stern tone and aspect, and said—

"One hundred dollars, for two nights' work! Do you take me for a fool? Here, fellow, is twenty dollars for you, and I consider you are well paid for your trouble."

"But sir," remarked Mike—"you know you promised—"

"Pooh!—promises are nothing; when a man wants to get possession of a pretty girl, he'll promise anything; when she is once in his power, he is not so liberal. Here, take your twenty dollars, and be off!"

"And this is my reward and thanks for the risk I have run!" demanded Jew Mike, bitterly.

"I've no time to waste words with you," rejoined Tickels, haughtily—"I know you; you're an old offender, and I could send you to prison, if I chose, without paying you a cent.—Once more, take the money, or leave it."

"Then you would break your contract with me? Be it so—keep your money; but, by God! I'll drink your heart's blood for this! My name is Jew Mike, and I have said it. Farewell, till we meet again!"

He rushed from the house, leaving Tickels divided by joy at having saved a hundred dollars, and fear, in consequence of the ruffian's savage threat.

Five minutes after Mike's departure, Corporal Grimsby entered, announced the abduction of Fanny Aubrey from the house of her friends, on the preceding night, and boldly accused Tickels of having been the cause of that outrage. The details of this interview are related in the sixth chapter of this narrative; it is consequently unnecessary to repeat them.

Satisfied in his own mind that old Tickels was at the bottom of the business, and that Jew Mike was the agent employed, the Corporal made the best of his way to Ann street, resolved to find the Jew, and prevail upon him, by bribes, to disclose the place where Fanny had been carried. During the whole of that day, he searched in vain; Mike was nowhere to be found;—towards evening, however, as the old gentleman was about to abandon the search in despair, he was informed by 'Cod-mouth Pat,' whom he had enlisted in his service, that Mike had just been seen to enter the

'Pig Pen.' With some difficulty, our friend contrived to gain an entrance to that 'crib,' where he had the satisfaction to find the object of his anxious search brooding over a half pint of gin. The ruffian instantly recognised in the Corporal, the person who had escaped from the 'Coal Hole,' some time previously, but every hostile feeling vanished, when the old man announced the object of his visit to be the discovery of Fanny Aubrey, and the punishment of the villain Tickels.

Without entering into details which might prove tedious, suffice it to say that Jew Mike agreed to conduct the Corporal to the place where Fanny was confined, on condition that the punishment of old Tickels should be left entirely to him, (Mike). This was assented to, and the pair instantly set out, in a cab, for the 'Chambers of Love,' in Warren street—the Corporal, eager to rescue poor Fanny from the power of her persecutors, and the Jew thirsting to revenge himself upon his employer, for having refused to give him the stipulated reward.

That same evening, at about the hour of seven, the Hon. Timothy Tickels issued from his residence in South street, and proceeded towards Warren street, which having reached, he entered the mansion of Madame Hearthstone. That lady, with a significant smile, conducted him to her chamber, and opened the secret panel; they descended the steps, and Mr. Tickels was ushered in the grand hall of the 'Chambers of Love.' The landlady pointed to the door of the apartment to which Fanny Aubrey had been conveyed; the old libertine opened the door, and entered.

In a few moments a piercing scream is heard—then another; but alas! those sounds could not be heard above, from the depths of that voluptuous tomb. But hark!—there is a noise without—nearer and nearer comes the tumult—the great door is burst open with a tremendous crash, and Jew Mike rushes in, followed by Corporal Grimsby. "This way!" shouts the Jew—"Forward!" responds the gallant Corporal. They reach the door of the *Satin Chamber*—they open it.

"Brick-bats and paving-stones! just in time again!"

There, upon a satin couch, her dress disordered and torn, her face flushed, her hair in wild disorder, her bosom naked and bleeding, lay Fanny Aubrey, panting, writhing, fiercely struggling in the ruffian grasp of the villain Tickels, who savagely turned and confronted the intruders. In an instant, he was stunned by a powerful blow from the gigantic fist of Jew Mike, and Fanny was folded in the arms of her preserver, the brave old Corporal.

They left that underground hell—the Corporal, bearing the now overjoyed Fanny in his arms, and Jew Mike, half carrying, half dragging the insensible form of old Tickels. They reached the chamber above, and emerged from the secret panel; the affrightened inmates of the house offered no resistance; they entered the cab which was in waiting, and were driven to the residence of the Corporal, who, with his fair young *protege*, alighted, and entered the house; then Jew Mike and his victim were driven to Ann street, and the vehicle halted before the cellar which led to the 'Pig Pen.'

The night was very dark, and no one observed the Jew, as, issuing from the cab, he descended into the cellar, bearing in his powerful arms the unconscious form of Tickels. Fortunately for him, he passed through the cellar and 'Pig Pen,' without exciting much notice, as the hour was too early for the usual revellers of the place to assemble, and those who saw him, merely supposed that he was carrying some drunken friend to a place of safety from the police—a sight common enough in that region. Mike needed no light to guide his footsteps, he traversed the dark passage, he seized the iron ring, and drew up the trap door of the 'Coal Hole,' from which the Corporal so providentially escaped. Then, with a deep curse, he cast the old libertine into the dark abyss, closed the entrance, and departed.

When Tickels revived, and found himself in that loathsome place, he rent the air with his cries and supplications; but no aid came to the crime-polluted wretch, and in a few days he sank beneath the combined effects of despair, starvation, and the foetid atmosphere, and miserably perished.

Conclusion

The Conclusion of a Tale is like the end of a journey: the Author throws aside his pen and foolscap as the tired traveller does the dusty garments of the road, and stretching himself at ease, looks back upon the various companions of his erratic ramblings.

The curiosity of the reader is doubtless highly excited to know who "Corporal Grimsby" is. Circumstances, we regret to say, will not permit us to state definitely—but should a guess be made that the worthy old Corporal, and a certain Capt. S——, commander of a Revenue Cutter, were one and the same person, we will venture to say that the conjecture would not be far removed from the actual truth.

The "Chevalier Duvall" and the "Duchess" still continue in their brilliant career of crime, in Boston. We regret that the limits of the present work have not permitted us to record more fully their extraordinary operations in voluptuous intrigue and stupendous fraud.

Fanny Aubrey is again a happy inmate of the family of Mr. Goldworthy. Poor Alice, although a shade has been cast over her pure life by the dark villainy of the Chevalier, has been restored to a state of comparative felicity by the constant kindness and sympathy of her relatives and friends.

"Jew Mike" has gone on a professional tour to the South and West. "Sow Nance" has become the most abandoned prostitute in Ann street.

Dear reader, thanking thee for the patience with which thou hast accompanied us in our devious wanderings, and hoping that thou hast not always found us to be a dull companion, we bid thee farewell.